YIELD TO ME

A Club Excelsior Novella

SARAH CASTILLE

NEW YORK TIMES BESTSELLING AUTHOR

Published by Sarah Castille

Print Edition
Cover by Croco Designs
ISBN: 978-0-9938168-1-9

This book was previously published in the *New York Times* Bestselling anthology, *Unraveled*, ISBN 9780991916 (no longer available for purchase), and now includes approximately 50% new content.

To Nana, and her secret love of romance

Chapter One

"YOU'RE AFRAID OF submission."

Kneeling astride a grapple dummy in the corner of the fight ring, primed and ready to test a new submission move, Marcy Foster frowned at the dark-haired stranger squatting beside her.

"Do I know you?"

"Jax Stratham. Fight coach and consultant. I'm here for the next six weeks to help Club Excelsior's fighters up their game. Didn't Reid tell you I was starting today?"

"Maybe." Reid Callaghan, the club's owner, probably had told her, but she rarely paid attention to the politics at Seattle's Club Excelsior. She was here to train, not socialize. Be the best damn MMA fighter possible. After disappointing her high-achieving family at every turn, she had finally found something she could do well, and if she won the Washington State Championship, she might be able to work up the nerve to tell them what she was doing with her life, possibly even make them proud.

"Maybe?" Jax frowned, the creases in his forehead doing nothing to mar his disturbingly handsome face, roughly chiseled to perfection. Seriously? What kind of fighter had a perfectly straight nose and not a single scar? And what was with the long hair? Thick and sable brown, just brushing the collar of his white Team Excelsior shirt, his hair invited touching … and pulling. There was a reason most fighters shaved their heads and why she French-braided her long brown hair before every fight.

Maybe he didn't fight anymore. Maybe he was just what he said. A coach.

"I don't need another coach." She dropped over the grapple dummy, positioning her elbows on either side of the dummy's head before she tucked her legs between the dummy's thighs.

Disturbingly life-like and covered with synthetic leather, the dummy had anatomically correct human features and joints but was missing a face and a male essential that could have made her solo fight practice more entertaining. At five feet four inches tall and weighing fifty pounds, the dummy was the smallest one in the gym, but then Marcy was one of the smallest fighters. Men outnumbered women ten to one at Club Excelsior, and there were only a handful of women training in the lower weight classes with her.

"You're part of the team. Reid says the team needs a push. You get me."

Marcy huffed and shifted position for an Ezekiel choke from inside the guard. "I'm four and oh by knockout in my last four fights. Doesn't get better than that. Which means, I don't need a push or a coach."

Jax dropped to his knees on the mat beside her and folded his arms over his chest, causing his impressive biceps to flex into tight, rounded peaks, straining the sleeves of his T-shirt. Surrounded by muscle every night at the gym, Marcy wasn't usually affected by the sight of yet another pair of pythons, but something about the way his muscles swelled against the hard planes of his chest sent a delicious shiver down her spine.

Or maybe it was the fact he couldn't take a hint.

"Thanks for stopping by." She dropped into the choke and turned her head away, waiting for him to leave. Instead, he leaned forward, so close she could feel his breath warm against her ear.

"I watched all your fights on DVD," he said. "I've read all your interviews. I've been through Reid's file. So far, you've been lucky. Not one of your opponents was strong on submission, but all it takes is one expert and you'll be down for the count. If you freeze up every time someone puts you in submission, you'll never have a shot at the state title."

Marcy swallowed hard and pushed herself up, treating him to a cold glare. "I don't freeze up." At least not every time. Her words sounded unconvincing, even to her. Could he sense the fear that had niggled at the back of her mind since Reid had first identified her problem—the possibility that maybe she wasn't cut out to be a fighter?

"Show me." His quiet demand caught her off guard, and she shot another glance at him from beneath the curtain of her lashes. His eyes were a soft brown, his lips perfectly sculpted, and his jaw square. Broad shoulders tapered to a slim waist, accentuating long, muscular thighs and a mouth-watering six-pack. But it was his sheer, palpable presence that gave her pause.

No. Not presence. Power. Raw power.

Her stomach fluttered. For the first time, her natural instinct to rebel failed. He spoke with confidence, an absolute certainty she would comply. The tenor of his voice was such that she doubted anyone ever disobeyed him.

"Ah…" She bit her lip to hide her internal disquiet and glanced down at the smooth, expressionless face of the practice dummy beneath her. "Grapple Man isn't very good for practicing submissions."

"Maybe not, but I am."

Marcy's heart thudded in her chest. "I've already practiced with a partner tonight. I don't think—"

"On your back. Legs apart. I'll mount and take the dominant position."

She startled at his abrupt command, and heat flooded her veins, pooling between her thighs. Flustered at her body's unexpected response to words she heard every day in practice, she stiffened. "Maybe another—"

Firm hands grasped her around the waist, lifting her off the grapple dummy and into the air. Although strong, she was a UFC flyweight at best, and he handled her as if she weighed nothing. Instinctively, she twisted to face him and kicked blindly, making contact, but instead of releasing her, Jax carried her down to the mat, then rolled until he had her on her back.

His hard, heavy body pinned her to the padded vinyl surface, his hips pressed tight against the juncture of her thighs. Shock stole her breath away. Okay, so maybe he wasn't *just* a consultant. She'd only seen moves like that in the pros.

"Breathe." His bourbon-smooth voice wound through her like a silken ribbon, loosening the tension that had frozen her lungs and releasing a wave of anger more intense than anything she had ever felt in the practice ring.

Who was he to manhandle her into submission? Who gave him the right to waltz in here and tell her she wasn't fighting her best fight? And why the hell was she trembling?

"Get off me." She pressed her hands against his rock-solid chest and pushed.

Jax grasped her wrists and leaned forward, pinning her hands to the mat above her head. "Make me."

She twisted and writhed beneath him, but despite her skill, he was simply too big, too strong, and too experienced to be thrown, countering her moves seamlessly with only the slightest adjustments to his hold. Marcy had never been so absolutely and overwhelmingly pinned. Even when she trained with the male fighters in the gym, they held back, giving her enough room to move, fight, and breathe. But Jax held nothing back. Whenever she found an inch of wiggle room—a lift of her shoulder, a turn of her thigh—he simply dropped his weight and tightened his hold.

She drew in a ragged breath and caught the scent of his cologne, sharp and fresh. Her mouth watered. So inappropriate. She should be angry and afraid. And yet it wasn't fear that sent adrenaline coursing through her veins, making her heart pound, but the profoundly erotic sensation of being trapped under his hot, heavy body, totally under his control.

Long-dormant arousal sent a pulse of desire down her spine, so intense she trembled, so deeply buried she almost didn't recognize it for what it was. But with it came the memory. Preston. Her heart squeezed, and she drew in a sharp, shuddering breath.

"You okay?" His brow wrinkled in consternation.

She gritted her teeth and shook off the memory, the self-loathing and disgust on Preston's face when he'd walked away, and her absolute sense of despair at having revealed her deepest, most secret desires only to be reviled by the one person she had thought would accept her for who she was.

"As okay as someone can be with two hundred pounds of muscle lying on top of them."

Jax laughed. "Let's even the odds." He slid his hand around her waist and rolled until he was on his back, with Marcy straddling his hips. The ease with which he manipulated her body was at once disconcerting and sublime.

She glanced quickly around the gym. Was anyone watching them? Would they think Jax's actions inappropriate? But although the gym was packed, all the cardio machines in use, line-ups at the free weights, mats full to capacity with fighters practicing grapple techniques, no one was looking in their direction. Well, except for Two Step.

She caught Two Step's gaze and shook her head when he took a step forward. Two Step frowned. One of the few superweights in the club, with a heart almost as big as his beautifully dark, barrel chest, Two Step had become her self-appointed guardian on her first day at Club Excelsior when he'd done her weight class assessment and pronounced her "baby size."

Turning away, she looked down at Jax. He

had folded his arms behind his head as if he were lounging on his couch instead of lying on the mats in an MMA gym with Marcy astride his hips.

Despite the intensity of his gaze and the probing questions he asked about her favorite moves and techniques, Marcy managed to hold up her end of the conversation while soaking in the feeling of his hard body between her thighs and raking her gaze over the taut lean muscle that rippled beneath his shirt when he shifted position. Once or twice, she made a move to slide off him, but Jax stayed her with the slightest shake of his head, telling her he preferred to have his intake meetings with new fighters in whatever position they felt most comfortable. And she seemed to be more comfortable sitting on him than most.

From there, they moved to basic grapple moves and techniques so Jax could assess her skill. For the first time ever in the ring, she felt clumsy and awkward, her arm bars and triangles almost laughably ineffective. But if Jax noticed, he gave no sign. Instead, he spent the next hour drilling her through the basics until her muscles had heated and relaxed, her breaths were coming in pants, and she had no thoughts beyond the moment he called it quits.

But, damn, he was good. And patient. Reid would have lost it with her by now, and the whole gym would have been privy to his irritation. By contrast, Jax's voice remained calm and even no matter how many times she had to repeat the moves until she got them right.

Finally satisfied with her basics, Jax lay back on the floor, motioning for Marcy to mount him. With a sigh, she straddled his abdomen and tightened her thighs around his hips.

"Now what?"

"Submission time." He gave her a breathtaking smile, and in one swift movement, he grabbed her left wrist and tugged her arm across her body, pressing her tricep against her carotid artery. His leg came up over her shoulders, hooking under his opposite shin in a basic triangle submission. He had only to increase the pressure of the hold to cut off her air and make her lose consciousness. A simple submission.

But effective.

Marcy froze and glared at his impassive face as her training kicked in. Bastard. This was totally unfair. He was twice her size and twice as strong. She lifted her head to preclude the full force of the submission and struggled to bring her arm away from her neck.

"Yield." Jax's lips twitched at the corners.

"Go to hell." She struggled in his hold, trying to find a way of reversing or escaping the figure-four lock, painfully aware of the proximity of her head to the generous bulge beneath his fight shorts that she prayed was a cup.

He increased the pressure on her throat by pulling her arm away from her body and pressing down with his leg. A warning.

"Yield, little fighter."

Fury overrode common sense. "No."

And then a shadow fell across the mat. Marcy glanced up into Reid's scowling face and groaned.

Six feet three inches of solid muscle with broad shoulders and lean hips, Reid had tattoos covering most of his massive back and chest.

Too handsome for his own good, his blond hair was cropped military short, and three hoop earrings glistened in his ear. No one messed with Reid. The once UFC pro heavyweight champ had retired after a severe knockout almost cost him his life, but he still kept up the same rigorous exercise regimen, and he ran the gym like a military boot camp.

"What's going on?"

"I don't need him." Marcy struggled in Jax's hold, but no matter what she did, she couldn't break his submission without rendering herself unconscious.

Reid squatted down beside her and tilted his head to the side. His lips quirked up in an amused smile. "Looks to me like you do."

"Get him off me."

"Tap out. Or have you suddenly forgotten how to fight?"

When Jax raised an eyebrow, she was tempted to refuse, but she didn't want to annoy Reid. She wouldn't be where she was without him, much less have a job at his family's sporting goods store, and although he would do anything for his fighters, he had a low threshold for disobedience in his club.

With an irritated sigh, she thumped the mat twice with her hand. Jax released her and swung his leg off her shoulders.

"Looks like you have some fight in submission after all." Jax winked, and Marcy pushed herself up, backing away until she was standing in the comfort of Reid's shadow.

Reid glanced from Marcy to Jax and back to Marcy. "Jax is the best fight consultant in the business. He's here for four weeks to help our team train for the state championships. Give him a chance. His methods are unorthodox, but he gets results. I won't let you throw away a promising career just because you don't like his techniques."

Marcy glanced over at Jax, leaning against the ropes, thick arms folded. Could she train with him? He had to be about six or seven years older than her, making him about thirty-one or thirty-two, and so damned handsome it was almost a sin. Why couldn't Reid have found a plain coach? Maybe an old, retired fighter, soft and slightly balding, with a bit of a paunch. Someone without a strong, toned body and lean, powerful legs. Someone she wouldn't want lying on top of her … dominating her.

Her breasts tingled with the memory of his hard chest pressed tight against her nipples and the ripple of smooth, warm skin over rock-hard muscle as she struggled to get free. But it was the raw power vibrating beneath the surface that set her blood on fire. Everything about him awakened feelings in her she had buried long ago. After Preston.

Jax's face softened. "You want to be the best, Marcy? You want to win the state championship? You can't be afraid of submission. You need to embrace it. Fight back. I know you're on the card to fight at TriStar's event next week. I promise I can make a difference in one week. Let me help you."

She held his gaze for a moment too long, a moment that made her heart pound and her mouth go dry. She didn't need the distraction, nor did she need his help. With a shrug, she turned away. "No, thanks."

✧ ✧ ✧

No.

He shouldn't have been surprised. After what he'd just seen in the ring, he should have realized Marcy wouldn't easily accept help. Reid would have known that about her. So why hadn't he warned Jax? He would have taken an entirely different approach. Not come on so strong.

Or maybe he should have come on stronger.

Jax stood beside Reid and watched Marcy cross the floor toward the exit, her beautiful ass perfectly outlined in her fight shorts. Damn, she was sexy. He'd trained lots of female fighters, but something about Marcy pushed all the right buttons. Like most serious female fighters, she was lean and toned, but she'd kept her curves in the places that mattered most. His groin tightened at the memory of her breasts pressed up against his chest, the swell of her hips as she sat astride him, her creamy thighs parting as she settled in full mount. Thank god he'd worn a cup, although if she'd remained on top of him even one second longer, the cup wouldn't have been much use in hiding his body's response.

"Marcy." Reid called her name, and she turned. Her gaze rested on Jax for the briefest second before flicking to Reid, but for that moment, he was lost again in that sparkling green sea. Such beauty. With her perfectly heart-shaped face, high cheekbones, and long, dark lashes, she'd almost totally distracted him from his task of assessing her response to submission.

His mind still reeled from their brief grappling session. Not so much from her skill in the ring but from the way she'd responded to his touch. For a brief few moments, she had submitted in an entirely different way—an unspoken plea that had triggered his dominant instincts.

Totally inappropriate. He was here as a coach and a teacher. Reid had brought him in to help Excelsior's fighters overcome the psychological barriers that were holding them back. With his background as a fighter and his experience as a psychologist, he had carved out a niche in the MMA coaching world that put his services in high demand. Reid had booked him over a year ago, and Jax's waiting list had doubled since then.

"You toe the party line or you walk," Reid called out to her, his voice carrying over the drum roll of speed bags, the slam of bodies on the mats, and the clank of weights. "I paid a lot of money to bring Jax to Seattle. The least you can do is to give him a chance."

Seemingly unembarrassed by Reid's indiscreet rebuke, Marcy shrugged. Then she turned and walked away.

Jax's lips quivered with a repressed smile. Marcy wasn't going to be pushed into doing anything she didn't want to do. Maybe she needed time to cool off. Reid clearly hadn't been forthcoming about his arrival. Still, in the brief time he'd spent with her, she'd come across as ambitious and determined. Why wouldn't she be interested in overcoming her issue with submission?

"You think she'll be back?" He looked over at a frowning Reid.

"I have no fucking idea." Reid scrubbed his hand over his face. "I don't know what just happened there. Maybe she didn't take on board the extent of your involvement when I mentioned to the team you were coming. You're the psychologist. What do you think?"

From her guarded reaction and the speed with which she'd turned down his offer of assistance, he thought she was afraid of something, but he wasn't about to tell Reid. "Hard to say. I've only just met her. But maybe the ultimatum wasn't a good idea."

Reid bristled. "My club. My team. My rules. She knows how I run things. Never been a problem before."

"You know her best."

"I'll talk to her." Reid pulled open the ropes and stepped out of the ring. "It took me a long time to convince her she has what it takes to be a fighter and even longer to convince her to train seriously. But she's good. Damn good. If she can just get over this one issue, I think she has what it takes to go pro."

From the fights he'd watched on DVD, Jax agreed. And he could help her achieve that goal. He'd just have to lock away the feelings she roused in him, the emotion that had surfaced when she'd responded to his touch. He was a professional, and he would keep it professional, no matter how beguiling she might be. And then he'd move on, as he always did. The psychologist in him acknowledged he was deep into avoidance and still running away. But in the end, he was just a man with a broken heart, trying to make it through each day.

Chapter Two

"HOW'S MY FAVORITE fighter and soon-to-be state champ?" Val Rosario, the assistant manager of Callaghan & Sons Sporting Goods, waved from the till as Marcy entered the store, ready for her afternoon shift. The Callaghan brothers had recently relocated the store to South Lake Union, only a few blocks away from Club Excelsior, and Marcy planned to follow as soon as she could save up enough money to rent an apartment in the area.

"Wishing you weren't on holiday the other day when I needed someone to talk to." Marcy mocked a frown as she shrugged off her coat. Val had been the Callaghan brothers' first hire. She knew everything about every piece of sporting equipment the store stocked. She also made it her business to know everything about the three Callaghan brothers who owned the store and the gym where they trained. Not that Val had ever been to the gym, but she was a fight fan and always stayed on top of the gossip.

"You should have come with me." Val stretched out her long arms to show off her tan. Tall and slim, with dark hair and warm, brown eyes, she already looked exotic, but the tan made her already-golden skin radiant. Marcy felt a twinge of regret at her decision not to join Val and their friends on an impromptu spring holiday to get away from the Seattle rain, but vacations were no fun when she couldn't drink and her menu choices were limited to protein and steamed veg so she could make weight at the upcoming event.

"I know."

"Nothing beats the Mexican Riviera for a low-cost, high-sun, hot-guy holiday."

Marcy's eyes widened. "You met some hot guys? Hotter than Brad?" Marcy and Val had become fast friends her first day on the job after they'd spent an afternoon drooling over the three Callaghan brothers as they put up new shelving. Val had given her a lecture about how to keep the Callaghan brothers in their place and then asked Marcy to choose which of the three bachelors she would take to bed (or two, if she was that way inclined).

Marcy had picked Reid, although Brad, the youngest brother, was more to her taste, with his mop of blond hair and a glint in his eye that suggested he'd been the hell-raiser of the family. But she'd seen the way Val watched him, and she hadn't wanted to upset her new friend. The oldest brother, Zack, the store manager, was out of the running. Tall and heavily built with a shaved head, a gruff voice, and a fierce scowl, he was intimidating even for a woman not easily cowed.

Val's shoulders sagged. "No one is hotter than Brad. And one day he'll dump that nasty piece of work he's been dating and realize what he's been looking for has been under his nose for years. But I did find a twosome who live in Oakland, Phil and Jack. I've set us up for Saturday night." She licked her lips and smiled. "Of course, I sampled the goods first. I hope you don't mind."

Laughter bubbled in Marcy's chest. Val was still on a mission to find her a man. Especially after Marcy had revealed she dated only casually and hadn't had a serious relationship for years. As a result, every few weeks, Marcy would be ambushed by yet another of Val's prospects as she stocked the shelves, and an awkward conversation would ensue with a man who was clearly not interested in camping gear, fight equipment, or baseball gloves.

"Tempting as it is to share your sloppy seconds times two, I'll have to pass," Marcy said. "Reid kicked me out of Excelsior, and I need to find a new place to train. I've got an event coming up—"

"Whoa." Val frowned. "Reid kicked you out? Reid, who can't take his eyes off you and tells everyone you're the next Ronda Rousey?"

Marcy's cheeks heated, and she grabbed her apron and joined Val behind the counter. "Yeah, well, he hired a hot new fight coach to get the team ready for the state championships, and the guy, Jax, he's just…"

"Hot?" Val tied Marcy's red apron around her waist and finished it off with a giant bow.

"Very."

"And that's a problem?" She spun Marcy around and handed her a pricing gun, then gestured toward the stock room, where Zack would, no doubt, be waiting for her with his usual scowl.

"He made me uncomfortable." Marcy sucked in her lips and took a quick look around to make sure Zack wasn't within earshot. "I couldn't focus on the training. He handled me like a doll, lifting me, turning me, putting me on top of him. I had no control, and I'm not weak by any means. I could move only when he let me move. Even when I'm practicing with the fighters, they hold back. Jax didn't. I've never been in that position before." But she'd dreamt about it. Fantasized about a man who could totally and utterly take control. Shared her desires with Preston only to have them thrown in her face.

The front door opened, and Marcy smiled when two fighters from Club Excelsior walked into the store. Although Callaghan's sold a wide variety of sporting equipment, Excelsior's fighters were their biggest customers.

Marcy waved them toward the back of the store. "Fight equipment. Aisle six."

Val waited until the fighters had disappeared down the aisle, then dropped her voice to a whisper. "So, what happened?"

"Reid said I had to train with Jax or leave. So I left." She feigned nonchalance although inside she was still reeling. Reid had called her in the morning, and when she hadn't been able to give him a good explanation why she didn't want to train with Jax, he had exploded and reiterated the ultimatum. She couldn't understand why he was being so difficult. In the end, it was her career. Sure, it helped to be part of a team, but when she stepped into the ring, it was her fight. Her win. Her loss.

Val shook her head. "You're both stubborn as mules. No wonder you two never got together. You can't leave the club. That club is your life. Your friends are there. Your fledgling fight career is there. And I can guarantee Reid doesn't really want you to leave. You know what he's like when he's backed into a corner."

Marcy shook her head. "It's not just that. There's something else going on with Reid. He wants me to train with Jax so badly I wonder if there's something he's not telling me about my fighting." Like she wasn't cut out for it, or that she'd never make it without serious help. Wouldn't that be ironic? Despite all her hard work, she would still be the failure her family had always thought she was.

"Nah." Val tied up her long, dark hair in a quick ponytail and then picked up her pricing gun. "Reid's straight up. He'll tell you what he's thinking even if you don't want to hear it. I'll bet by tonight he'll tell you he's sorry and wants you back in the club."

"I've never heard him say sorry."

Val's smile faded, and she turned away, her voice dropping to a soft murmur. "I have."

A steady stream of customers kept them busy until midafternoon. When they finally got a break, Val went to the storeroom to check the new deliveries, and Marcy returned to the mind-numbing task of pricing a shipment of baseball gloves. Five years ago, working at the sporting goods store had seemed a good way to indulge her love of sports and show her parents she wasn't interested in a Wall Street career. But now that the novelty had worn off and she was effectively estranged from her family, she often found herself longing for something more.

"Marcy."

She spun around and then froze when she recognized Jax in the doorway. Swallowing hard, she slapped a sticker on a glove and tried to play it cool, as if the sound of his voice didn't make her body heat in an instant, or as if she hadn't been up most of the night fantasizing about what would have happened if they'd been alone in the ring.

"Hey, Jax." Her voice rose in pitch despite her best attempts to keep it level. "You looking for some equipment?"

His eyes roved over her body, and she stiffened and cleared her throat. Jax met her gaze, amusement in his eyes. "Never seen you in regular clothes. Marcy without the armor. Soft and sweet."

Burn, cheeks. Burn. "Never seen you in regular clothes, either. You look … good."

Now there was an understatement. With his gray Club Excelsior T-shirt stretched tight over his broad chest and his jeans hugging his narrow hips, he was beyond mouth-watering. Good thing she'd already had lunch.

Flustered, she twisted her ponytail around her finger. "So, what are you looking for?"

"You."

"Me?"

"I wanted to talk to you about coming back to the club and training with me if I can get Reid to back down on his ultimatum."

Marcy snorted and slapped a tag on another glove. "Won't happen."

"One of you has to back down." His voice dropped, and he covered her free hand with his own. The pricing gun fell to the counter, and she looked up and lost herself for the briefest moment in the depth of his warm brown eyes.

"Not me."

He rubbed his thumb over her knuckles, sending bolts of white lightning zinging to her core.

"Why are you so adverse to training with me?"

His touch, the scent of his cologne, the deep rumble of his voice, and the heat emanating from his perfect body all converged in a rush of sensation that fuzzed her brain and allowed the truth to slip from her lips before she could catch it. "Because of this."

Jax stilled, his face smoothing into an expressionless mask. "You like my touch?"

Her cheeks flushed, and she looked away. "I just think it would be difficult to train with you and…" She bit her lip, unused to being so candid about her feelings, especially with someone she barely knew. "Stay focused."

He squeezed her hand. "I had that problem, too."

Marcy's head jerked up. "So you agree. Maybe if you tell Reid you think—"

"No, I don't agree," he said, cutting her off.

"I think I can help you with your training. But maybe we should talk about finding a way around what seems to be a mutual attraction."

Oh god. He'd just thrown it out there. Good to know her feelings weren't one-sided, but she'd never met anyone who just laid it on the line. No coy gestures or subtle glances. No wondering what he thought. He'd laid his hand on the table, and now it was her turn to play.

"I'm at work." She cringed as soon as the inane words left her lips. He knew she was at work. She was pricing gloves behind the counter with a big red Callaghan's Sporting Goods apron tied around her waist.

Jax's eyes glittered, amused. "After work then. What time do you get off?"

"Six."

"I'll pick you up at six, and we'll go for dinner." A statement, not a question, but she liked the way he took control. Maybe too much.

"Okay."

"I also need to pick up some equipment." He smiled, and his face softened. "I had more than one reason to come here today."

Marcy's tension eased. "What are you looking for?"

"Tape, a mouth guard, practice gloves, and a cup."

For a long moment, she forgot to breathe. *Oh god no.* No images of cups and where they might go. No thoughts of Jax's cup digging into her ass when she sat astride him in the ring.

Swallowing hard, she pointed behind him. "Aisle six."

"You want to take this customer, Marcy? I'll handle the till." Val appeared out of nowhere, swooping down on them with a smirk that left Marcy in no doubt she'd been eavesdropping on their conversation.

"Um…" Marcy looked over at the two fighters behind Jax, waiting to pay. "I have other customers."

Ignoring Marcy's pointed glare, Val waved Marcy away from the counter. "I'll handle them. You go ahead. Take him where he needs to go. Show him the goods." She winked, and Marcy resolved never to speak to her betraying friend again.

"Aisle six, isn't it?" Jax gave her a warm smile. "You can talk me through the products, and we can finish our conversation."

With a defeated sigh and a last irritated glance at Val, she tossed the pricing gun on the counter. "Fine. Follow me."

Two agonizing minutes of Jax's eyes boring into her back later, they arrived at aisle six. Marcy led Jax past the grapple dummies and punch bags to the men's clothing section. Fight shorts hung in neat rows along the wall, and packaged cups filled the shelves.

"Here they are." She waved her hand over the display and tried not to think of where Jax might place a cup and what might go in it. "In the shorts or out?" Most of the male fighters she knew preferred bike-style compression shorts with a built-in pouch for a cup, but some still preferred the extra protection afforded by a full groin protector.

"I don't know. How rough are you planning to be with me? Last time, I had a narrow escape."

She looked at him aghast. "You weren't … wearing anything?"

Jax captured her with his gaze, and his voice dropped husky and low. "Don't usually need it when I'm coaching, but with you…"

Her cheeks flushed red. "Um, since I'm not planning on making any … direct contact, I'd recommend the fight-short style."

"You're embarrassed." He raised an eyebrow, and his lips twitched with a smile. "Haven't you sold cups to your friends before?"

Get a grip. Marcy willed the flush out of her cheeks, breathing in the comforting scent of plastic and latex and a faint whiff of leather. "Sure. All the time."

He closed the distance between them and stroked a finger over the apple of her burning cheek. "So why are you blushing?"

She met his curious gaze. "They weren't … you know … my coach."

"What's wrong with your coach?"

He was so close now she could feel the heat of his body through her clothes. God, he was sexy. Too sexy. The kind of sexy that usually sent her running out the door.

"Nothing." Her voice came out in a whisper.

"Wrong." He cupped her cheek, tracing

along the curve of her jaw with his thumb, burning a trail across her skin, his gaze intent, focused. "I came to set things right between you and Reid and convince you to train with me, and yet somehow I wound up asking you out for dinner. But dinner isn't really what I want."

"We don't have to—"

Jax leaned down and pressed his lips to her ear. "I want you, Marcy. Like no one I've ever wanted before. It makes no sense since we've only spent a few hours together, and I'm mindful of my responsibilities as a coach. But I won't pretend I didn't feel something when we were on the mats last night. Something I want to explore with you."

Marcy's breath caught in her throat as adrenaline surged through her veins. He just assumed she felt the same, expected she would want to explore their explosive sexual chemistry, too. And he was right. Six o'clock couldn't come soon enough.

His lips slid over her cheek, and then his mouth touched hers, light as a feather but with the impact of one of Two Step's signature punches.

"Later."

Her breath left her in a rush, and although she knew she should pull away, she leaned up to kiss him back. But she was a second too late.

"Got a bunch of customers up front who need some help." Val's voice cut through the stillness as she leaned against the shelf at the end of the aisle. Her gaze flicked to Jax and then back to Marcy. "'Course, I could always handle them myself."

"No, we're done here." Marcy pushed past Jax and headed down the aisle, struggling to steady her senses.

What the hell had she been thinking? She'd just kissed Jax.

Her coach.

Reid would kill her if he ever found out. Talk about not taking her training seriously.

But still…

She touched her fingers to her mouth, still warm and sweet from Jax's lips, and then glanced at her watch.

Five hours until six o'clock.

Five. Long. Hours.

Chapter Three

IT WAS WRONG to want her.

He knew this, even as he watched her cross the street toward him, her body moving with the easy grace of a professional athlete, her hair, now loose, spilling around her shoulders in glorious chestnut waves.

And yet, here he was, leaning against his vehicle, feet planted firmly on the ground, his body thrumming with anticipation. Over the last five hours, he had resolved not to give in to his baser desires. He wanted to get to know her. Talk to her. Find out what lay behind the problem Reid had said was becoming a serious impediment to her career.

"Sushi or steak?" He knew she had an event coming up and, like all fighters, to ensure she made her weight class, she had to watch her diet carefully, which meant protein, vegetables, and protein shakes.

Marcy lifted an eyebrow. "I thought you didn't want dinner."

Jax swallowed hard. How the fuck was he going to maintain his resolve now? But he should have known. Although he suspected she was submissive in the bedroom, there was nothing submissive about the woman standing in front of him dangling a set of keys from her hand. This was fighter Marcy—a woman who knew what she wanted and wasn't afraid to go after it. But for a moment in aisle six, she'd shown him a different side of herself. A softer side. And damned if he didn't want both.

"Where?"

"My place." She handed him a piece of paper. "I'll meet you there."

Jax watched her leave, her hips swaying with her confident stride. Damn, what a woman. When she turned the corner, he stepped into his rental car and plugged her address into his GPS. Unless she was planning to cook, it seemed dinner was off the agenda.

With no idea how the evening would go and no plan beyond spending some time with Marcy, he arrived at her house uncharacteristically edgy. As a result, he was taken aback and less than gracious when Reid greeted him at the door.

"Reid."

"Hey, Jax. Marcy said you might stop by."

Jax gritted his teeth and forced himself to shake Reid's extended hand, then followed Reid into the house in a semi-state of confusion.

"Looks like we both had the same idea about changing Marcy's mind." He offered Jax a beer, but Jax declined and shot a questioning glance at Marcy, leaning against the doorjamb. Did she and Reid live together? How had he so badly misjudged the situation?

Marcy shrugged. "Reid was waiting outside. Two surprise visitors in one day. I've never been so popular."

Jax's tension eased. Okay. Unexpected visit. Still, it was goddamned disappointing.

Reid stretched out on Marcy's couch, a plush blue three-seater with an easy chair to match.

Her house was neat and uncluttered, the decor simple, elegant, but lacking in the personal touches he expected to see in a home. Jax looked around the open-plan living room and dining room of the modern townhouse, and his gaze fell on the closet. He suspected if he opened that door, the real Marcy would spill out. Or maybe she saved her real self for the bedroom.

"So, let's get down to business." Reid took a swig of his beer, and his hand swayed over the table when he went to place it down. Only then did Jax realize Reid had been drinking.

"I paid a hell of a lot of money to bring Jax here, and mostly for you." Reid pointed at Marcy, and her eyes widened.

"Me? Why didn't you talk to me about it first? If you thought the problem was serious enough to bring someone in, you should have let me know. I thought it was just a minor issue."

"Life or death." Reid leaned forward and steadied himself on the arm of the couch. "It's a life-or-death problem. I didn't want to tell you how serious it was 'cause I didn't want to make it worse, and for a while, I thought we were working through it. Every second you delay getting out of a submission hold increases your chances of injury exponentially, not to mention costing you the fight. I thought I could help you, but it's not a physical problem; it's psychological, and Jax is a psychologist."

Marcy frowned. Jax knew that frown. He saw it all the time when people thought he was secretly assessing them and finding them wanting, or when he came up against the widely held belief that psychologists only treated sick people.

"You're a psychologist?"

He nodded. "Used to be a pro fighter but gave it up to make use of my degree and coach."

Even if Marcy hadn't sucked in her lips and taken a step back, Jax would have sensed her withdrawal. As if the woman who had dangled her keys on the street, her eyes gently teasing, had gone to ground, and he was left with the public Marcy. Calm, cool, collected, and detached. "I don't need a psychologist. There's nothing wrong with me."

"No one thinks there is."

She bristled and turned to the kitchen. "Apparently you both do or you wouldn't be here."

"Fuck." Reid thumped his feet on the coffee table after the kitchen door banged behind her. "She's not gonna change her mind."

"Not when you brought it up like that." Jax couldn't keep the bitterness from his voice. For a club owner, coach, and one-time fighter, Reid seemed unable to understand the particular sensitivities of his fighters. Jax had been at the club only a short time, and already he could see Reid's heavy hand in almost every fighter's training. A more nuanced approach would bring out the best in everyone, an understanding of latent issues or psychological blocks. But Reid had trampled over all but the most obvious skill-related concerns, and his fighters were suffering for it.

"If you want my professional opinion," he said, taking a seat across from Reid, "let her return to the club. Even if she joins another gym, it could take her up to a year to build the level of trust she needs in her training partners, and her career will suffer for it. I'll be around for the next few weeks if she changes her mind, and if not, she'll need you. A new coach isn't going to understand the problem the way you do. He won't be able to help."

Reid nodded, appeased by Jax's flattery. "Sounds like a plan. I'll tell everyone she didn't need your help. Save face." He pushed himself to his feet and rubbed his hands together. "Looks like our work here is done. How 'bout we go out for a coupla drinks? Marcy's pissed at us, and she can't drink anyway, so sticking around here will be as much fun as watching paint dry."

Jax's stomach clenched. God, how had an evening of such promise turned out so badly? Spending an evening with Reid was about the last thing he wanted to do.

"Let me talk to Marcy first." He crossed the room and stepped into a bright, modern kitchen with dark wood cupboards, stainless steel appliances, and granite counters. Marcy was at the island chopping vegetables, each slice of her knife hitting the cutting board in firm rebuke.

"You okay?"

She looked up and scowled. "You tell me.

You're the psychologist. Am I crazy for wanting to be a fighter? Do I have what it takes, or I am mentally fucked up?"

"That's not fair." He crossed the tile floor and put his hands on the counter in front of her. "Psychologists help people confront or deal with issues that may be too challenging for them to handle themselves. You aren't sick or crazy, and to be honest, I dislike when people react that way."

Immediately contrite, her face softened. "I'm sorry. It's just … a bit of a shock."

"Totally understandable." He reached for her hand in sympathy, and she jerked away.

"Don't touch me."

"Why?"

She leaned against the opposite counter, arms folded, the chopping knife still in her hand. "I don't want to be touched."

His heart squeezed in his chest. One step forward and two steps back. Well, Reid was right about one thing. Marcy didn't want company. "I'm going to take Reid home. He's in no shape to travel by himself, and I don't trust him in a taxi. He would probably pay the driver to take him to the nearest open bar."

Marcy resumed her chopping. "He doesn't drink very often, but when he does, watch out." She looked up and gave him a weak smile. "Thanks for looking after him."

"He's going to let you come back to the club. You don't have to train with me."

Marcy put down the knife and drew in a ragged breath, as if a burden had been lifted from her shoulders. "Thanks for that, too."

"Pleasure." He turned away, pausing at the door to look back over his shoulder at the woman who, only hours before, had tried to entice him into her bed. "Guess I'll see you at the event on Saturday."

Her eyes glistened, and she dipped her head. "Guess so."

Marcy adjusted her padded helmet and leaned against the ropes in her corner as Reid adjusted her gloves. The crowd seated in bleachers and chairs around the ring in the Cirque Events

Center was scant, at best. Her fault for agreeing to a showcase fight for a debut MMA organization in the Bay area. In an attempt to attract a wider audience, the new organization, TriStar, had pitted her against a Muay Thai specialist, Jenny Li, for a bout showcasing the different fighting styles in a five-rope ring.

Marcy preferred the ring to the cage for its openness and the illusion of freedom that came with it, but cage fighting was all the rage, and if she wanted a serious career, she had to up her cage fighting game. Still, she wasn't about to turn down the opportunity for some competitive practice, especially when her opponent was a striker, which meant Marcy wouldn't have to worry about the submission issue that arose primarily when fighters hit the mats and tried to keep each other down.

Reid put in her mouth guard and ran his hands down her body, checking to make sure there were no loose threads or tags on her silky red fight shorts. His hands slid lower, checking her shin pads and the wraps under her instep. Some fighters preferred to go without the padding, but Marcy had learned her lesson after a bout that had left her with bruises so bad she couldn't train for a week.

At the sound of the whistle, she stepped into the center of the ring and touched gloves with her opponent to start the fight. Li opened orthodox with an outside leg kick, which Marcy easily deflected. She returned with a jab when Li moved in, but her next punch went wide. Already breathing heavily, Marcy tried a front kick but wasn't fast enough to avoid Li's double underhooks. She doubled over as Li's fists slammed into her. *Damn.* Double score for Li.

Stomach aching, Marcy used the ropes to pull herself up, but Li was behind her. Li turned into her again and took her down. Marcy heaved herself up and connected two lefts, but Li picked her up for a slam and thumped her down on the mat. She flipped to her front, but Li was already down and on Marcy's back, her elbow around Marcy's throat as she attempted a rear naked choke. So much for strikers not being big into submission.

Marcy struggled, but Li only sank in deeper.

She could hear the deep timbre of Jax's voice from the ropes, and Reid's loud shouts. What were they saying? Did they want her to tap out? Were they telling her not to freeze? Well, they were wasting their time. There wasn't anything wrong with her, and once she got out of this damn submission hold, she'd prove it.

A tightening in her chest was the only warning she got that maybe Reid was right, after all. And then the world faded to black.

"Back in bed."

Bare legs dangling over the side of the hospital bed, gown bunched up around her thighs, Marcy froze mid escape when Two Step's voice boomed through her tiny hospital room.

He frowned when she caught his gaze. "I knew you wouldn't be able to sit still once you woke, so I told Reid and Jax I'd stand guard. Looks like I was right. Climb back into bed, baby girl. You aren't going anywhere. This is your punishment for not tapping out of that rear naked chokehold and losing consciousness."

Marcy gave him a weak smile, but with her head still fuzzy and her lips dry, she couldn't engage in their usual banter about the irritating nickname he had given her that had spread like wildfire through the club.

Two Step's smile faded in the silence, and his corded neck tightened as he swallowed. "You're supposed to tell me off for callin' you a baby girl. And then I'd tell you that you looked like a baby girl to me, all tucked up in that hospital bed for the last few hours."

Catching her gaze drifting to the water jug, he poured a glass of water and held the straw while she sipped. The cool water soothed her parched throat, and she slid back on the bed and leaned against the pillow with a sigh.

"You'd make a terrible jailer. You're far too nice."

He brushed a stray curl off her forehead, his gentle touch belying his massive frame. "More like relieved. You went down pretty hard."

The memory came back to her in a rush. Jenny Li's arm around her neck, slowly tightening. Reid and Jax shouting from the ropes. The moment when she froze instead of fighting back. And then blackness.

"It was nice of you to come," she said. "And it would be even nicer if you could break me out."

Two Step gave her a crooked grin as he paced back and forth in front of her bed, clearly restless in the stark, confined space. "You think anything would have kept me away? You've been in my corner for every fight. Least I can do is give you a pretty face to wake up to. Reid said you weren't close with your family."

Marcy shifted in the bed to face him, wincing as the IV tugged at her wrist. "As close as a black sheep can be. Sometimes I wonder if I was switched at birth. They're all academically inclined. High achievers. My brother and sister preferred schoolwork to sports and killed themselves to make it onto Wall Street like my parents. But all I ever wanted was to be outside kicking a ball around or climbing trees or jogging down by the Bay. They were pretty disappointed with my pot-smoking, class-skipping, party-until-you-drop death metal phase in high school and devastated when I went into retail and bought a dog instead of a cat. Total disappointment. I can't imagine what they'd think if I told them I was a fighter."

"You got a rebellious streak in you." Two Step patted her hand. "That's why the kids at the youth club love your fight classes. They sense you're one of them."

A smile tugged at Marcy's lips. She loved her Saturday mornings at the youth club with Two Step, teaching self-defense to kids who had to defend themselves every day on the street. "More like a sporting streak. My love of sports made me the family freak."

His face softened. "At Excelsior, we're all freaks one way or another."

She snorted a laugh and looked around for her clothes. "So how about letting a fellow freak escape? Now that the fight is over and I don't have to worry about making weight, I'm desperate for a hot dog and a chocolate fudge sundae."

"No can do." Two Step shook his head. "You aren't allowed to leave until you get the doc's all clear, and then you gotta deal with Reid."

"What do you mean, 'deal with him'?" Marcy frowned.

His jaw tightened. "He took it hard when you went down. Real hard. Like I thought he was gonna bust a vein. Says it's his fault for not picking up on that weakness a long time ago. Now he's banging the drum about you training with Jax." His voice broke, and he took a deep breath. "You might have been hurt worse if Jax hadn't been watching so closely. He was in the ring before you hit the floor…"

"I'll think about it."

Two Step frowned. "Is that a yes? It better be a yes. I don't think I could watch something like that again, baby girl. I know it happens to fighters all the time, but I can't watch it happen to you. And neither can Reid." He swallowed hard. "He cares about you, Marcy. A lot."

Marcy nodded. Reid had never hidden his interest in taking their friendship further. But although she liked him and was indebted to him for both her job and her fight career, he was too straight for her. She suspected Reid had never skipped classes, smoked pot on the school roof, or sneaked out of the house for an all-night rave when he was a teenager. And although she trained with him on a daily basis, she'd never once felt her body tingle the way it had when Jax had put her in submission.

A choice that was no choice. She didn't want to leave her friends and train at another club. Even the few days thinking she would have to leave had been torture. If she wanted to stay with the team, she would have to train with Jax, which meant locking away her silly fantasies and maintaining the same professional distance she had with her other coaches. And that was the key. He was a coach. Nothing more.

Chapter Four

PROFESSIONAL. KEEP IT PROFESSIONAL.

Jax leaned against the ropes in the practice ring as he watched Marcy cross the floor toward him, stopping along the way to talk with her friends. She'd agreed to train with him, but in an awkward conversation in the hospital, she'd laid down the line. Nothing personal. What had happened between them was all that was going to happen.

Just as well. He was already losing his professional detachment. His stomach had twisted when he'd seen her go limp in Jenny Li's hold, and although he wasn't authorized to be in the ring, he hadn't been able to stop himself from running to her aid the moment the referee blew the whistle. Reid had been only a step behind him.

Given that knockouts happened all the time in the MMA world, he had overreacted, but then so had Reid, which said a lot about his feelings for Marcy. Well, Jax wouldn't get in his way. He had already set up his next contract in Miami, starting in a few weeks. He'd get the job done and say his good-byes—as he always did. He touched his hand to his chest, an almost unconscious gesture of remembrance for his mother and sister and the good-byes that had broken his heart.

Problem was, he had to find a way to deal with the tightening in his gut every time he saw her—an uncharacteristic yearning. Yes, she was beautiful and sexy as sin. And Reid had been right about her skill. When she'd stepped into the ring at the TriStar event, he'd been blown away by her raw talent. She'd fought smart, and she'd fought hard. But then it had all gone to hell.

Well, it wouldn't happen again. Not on his watch.

Marcy reached the elevated ring and looked up at him, her soft green eyes wide with apprehension, the slightest flush in her cheeks. His abdomen tightened, and arousal stirred low in his groin.

So much for resolve.

He held the ropes open, and she joined him in the practice ring.

"White Sox fan?" She gestured toward the white lettering on his T-shirt.

"Always. Never missed a game when I was a kid. Some of my greatest memories are the afternoons I spent with my dad in the stadium. Those were the days I could eat hot dogs without worrying about making weight for my next event."

Her face brightened when she smiled. "I'm a White Sox fan, too, although I just go for the junk food and men in tight pants."

Jax chuckled. "I'm surprised Reid lets you eat junk food."

"He doesn't, but I'm not always so good at following the rules, as you'll find out tonight. If you're planning on tossing me around the ring again, I won't be so easy on you this time."

He saw her humor for what it was. An attempt to diffuse the tension. Still, he liked this side of her. Soft, gently teasing. He wanted more.

"I'll be sure to keep up my guard."

As he led her to the center of the ring, he caught her taking a quick glance around. The gym was busy for a Friday night. Every station had a line-up, from the free weights to the grapple mats and from the practice rings to the studios. The slap of gloves on leather, the steady beat of the punching bag, the *slip slap* of jump ropes, and the whirr of exercise machines all blended into a symphonic cacophony of sound. Was she glad for the company or wishing they were alone, as he did?

"Sit." He gestured to the mat, and they sat facing each other. Her fight shorts rode up as she crossed her legs, and he dragged his gaze away from the creamy softness of her inner thighs.

"Do you like to be touched?"

The question startled her as it was meant to do, and she blushed. "I don't understand—"

"It's a simple question. Do you like to be

touched? After watching you fight, I don't think you do."

Her voice dropped to a throaty rasp, and she looked away. "No. But I don't see how this is relevant to…"

He edged closer to her and took her hands in his. "That's what we're going to do tonight. I'm going to touch you. Not in a sexual way. Clothed areas are off limits. But I want you to get comfortable enough with touch that it doesn't elicit a fear response. Does that make sense?"

She shook her head. "Other fighters touch me every day in practice. I don't have a problem with that."

"But in a highly charged situation, when the adrenaline is flowing and you're being pressed into submission, you do. What I'm trying to figure out is whether you freeze because of the touch, the loss of control, or something else entirely." He helped her to her feet and led her over to one of the four corner pillars that marked the corners of the practice ring. "Face the pillar, hands on the ropes on either side."

For a long moment, she hesitated, and his

heart thudded in his chest. He could help her, wanted to help her, but more than that, he needed to help her. Some part of him had connected with her the first day they'd met, sensed a need in her that he knew instinctively he could fill.

She drew in a deep, shuddering breath and then placed her hands on the ropes.

A familiar warmth suffused his body, slowing his pulse and easing his tension. This was why he had left the ring and become a coach. He could help people in a way he had been unable to help his mother and sister. Never again would he feel that sense of helplessness and loss as he'd watched them die.

"Is this okay?" The slight sway of her body betrayed her anxiety, and he placed his hands on her shoulders to steady her.

"Relax, little fighter." He brushed his fingertips along her arm from shoulder to wrist, savoring the soft warmth of her smooth skin as a wave of heat crashed through his body. Christ. If he reacted like this every time he touched her, he would combust before the session ended.

Stepping back, he stripped off his shirt, but the cool air did nothing to dampen the fire raging through his veins.

Before he could stop her, Marcy spun around. "What are you—?" Her gaze fixed on his chest, and she sucked in a sharp breath.

"Awesome tats." She gestured to the intricate swirls inked across his pecs. "Is that a Celtic design?"

Jax steeled himself against the urge to press her hand against his chest and nodded. "My Dad is Irish. Some of the symbols are in our family crest."

"And the names?"

His breath caught as her finger hovered over his heart.

"My mother and sister. They died of breast cancer within five years of each other." With a gentle touch, he drew her hand away.

"Oh, Jax. I'm sorry."

Resting his hands on Marcy's shoulders, Jax turned her to face the post, taking a moment to regain his composure. Her genuine sympathy stirred emotions he went to great pains to hide.

"Back to work." He resumed the touching exercise with brusque, efficient movements, wondering what had possessed him to share such a personal piece of information. He usually kept his fighters at a distance, never socialized outside the gym. He wasn't there to make friends, especially when he knew, after a few weeks, he would be moving on to his next contract. And he and Marcy had come to an agreement.

Yet, as his hands glided over her body, her responsiveness drove away the momentary melancholy, replacing it with raw desire. He noted her every sharp intake of breath, the quiver of her muscles, and the heat of her skin. When she finally spoke again, he heard an unmistakeable waver in her voice, a need that matched his own.

"Jax … what are people going to think?"

"They'll think it's that crazy Jax training Marcy with his crazy ways." His fingers glided over the dip between her neck and shoulder blade, and a sliver of delight wormed its way into his chest when her breath hitched.

"And if it's Susie," he said, "she'll wish she were you because I made her stand on her head for half an hour this afternoon whistling 'Always Look on the Bright Side of Life.'"

Marcy laughed, and the last remnants of his sorrow drifted away.

"I didn't take you for a man with a sense of humor."

He rubbed his knuckles over her cheek. "And I didn't take you for a woman who didn't like to be touched."

"I wasn't always like this." Her voice was so soft he could barely make out her words, but he noted how tightly she clenched the rope with her fists when his finger traced over her collarbone, the quickening of her breaths. A disconnect between wanting to be in control and needing to let go.

"How did you get into fighting?" He moved closer, a distraction and a message. Here. Now. She didn't have to struggle. He was in control.

Marcy drew in a ragged breath. "It's not that interesting."

"Everything about you interests me, Marcy."

He slid his hands down her back, brushing over the bare skin between her sports bra and fight shorts and then sliding around to the front. He had done this exercise countless times and on many fighters, but here … now it seemed less an exercise and more an indulgence. Or even … an invitation.

His thumbs glided over her rib cage and abdomen, then along the waistband of her fight shorts, sending the wrong signals to the right part of his body.

So soft. So hot. So hard.

Stop.

With a mental jerk, he brought his mind back to his task, focusing on the mundane details of his life to quench his growing arousal: the reports he had to prepare for Reid, the renovations he had to complete to put his parents' house up for sale, the stray pup he'd found on the beach and given to his dad to help bring him out of his depression, the protein shake he'd had for lunch when really all he'd wanted was a couple of hamburgers in soft, white buns…

Fuck.

He crouched behind her and ran his fingers lightly down the backs of her toned legs and then up along the sensitive skin of her inner thighs. Marcy gasped and tightened her grip on the ropes.

"I'm still waiting to hear about how you became a fighter."

"I … ah … needed a job." Her voice was hoarse, delightfully throaty. "Reid's family owns a sporting goods store, and his brother hired me. A few weeks after I started, a man came in and tried to steal some watches. I didn't really think. I just reacted. It's one of my biggest problems, being impulsive. I chased him and knocked him to the ground. Got in a couple of punches before Reid caught up with us. He thought I might make a good fighter, so he brought me to the gym. Here I am."

Chuckling, Jax pushed himself to his feet. He could well imagine Marcy chasing down a thief. He'd seen her fire—her spark—the first day they'd met. "Sounds pretty exciting to me." He stroked his thumb up and down her neck, gently at first and then with increasing pressure until a soft “oh” escaped her lips.

“You like that.” Curious, he turned her around to study her face. Under his steady gaze, she blushed and looked away, but not before he caught the slight dilation of her pupils. Was her arousal a result of the exercise or the tiny jolt of pain, or both?

Or neither?

“So, how did you become a coach?” Her gaze drifted away from him and over to Reid, doing bicep curls in front of the mirror.

He swallowed an unexpected sliver of annoyance. “I was running away. Still am.” He caressed her cheek then cupped her jaw in his hand, tilting her head, forcing her to look at him as he leaned in…

“Jax?”

Chest heaving, jaw tight, he wrenched himself away, holding on to his control with the slimmest of threads. Too much. Too overwhelming. He had to cut it short or he would do something he would regret.

“We’re done for today. Same time tomorrow.”

As he stepped out of the ring, he wondered how he would make it through tomorrow. Hell, how would he make it through the night?

He plunged two fingers into her pussy. "So wet, baby," Jax whispered as he angled his fingers to pulse against her sensitive inner walls. "But I want you wetter."

Marcy arched out of her bath as she thrust two fingers deep inside her. With her other hand, she cupped her breast, then pinched her nipple between her thumb and forefinger.

Oh god. So close.

She closed her eyes and imagined Jax covering her with his body like he'd done in the ring. Except now he was naked, his broad chest glistening with sweat, his beautiful tattoos shining in the dim light as his cock, hard and thick, prodded at her entrance.

"I want to fuck you, Marcy. I want to fuck you till you scream."

She pumped her hand, spreading her fingers, pressing her palm against her clit, imagining his cock swelling inside her. But as she climbed toward her peak, her fantasy changed, and Jax had her facing the wall, her cheek pressed against the cool surface, hands bound and secured over her head. And then she heard the soft hiss of a flogger as its tails flew through the air. When the first imaginary blow thudded on her skin, she climaxed. Hard and fast. Pleasure merging with a fantasy pain. And then she sank into the water, drifted, wondering how she would tell Jax the training wasn't going to work.

A run in the park followed by an early-morning exercise routine cleared her head after a restless sleep. But the minute she saw Val at the store, something cracked inside her. Between the rows of boxing gloves and volleyballs, she let everything spill out: her desire for Jax and her fear for the future of her career.

Val thought she should sleep with Jax and get him out of her system. Then she wouldn't be wondering about how good he might be in bed; she'd know. Marcy didn't agree. Her career was at stake. What if sleeping together ruined their professional relationship? He was uniquely qualified to help her, and without his help, she might never get ahead. Val thought the sexual tension was already ruining their professional relationship, especially after Marcy told her how Jax had abruptly cut their last session short. And did Marcy ever consider that they might be able to make it work? Lots of relationships started in the gym. Lovers helped each other train. Why was she so different?

Marcy couldn't tell Val why she was different. She had never told anyone about her darkest, most forbidden fantasies—the fantasies she strongly suspected could come true in Jax's arms. He was simply the most dominant man she'd ever met. Where Reid was loud and aggressive when he wanted something done, Jax could command obedience solely through the tone of his voice, a look, or even a touch. Utterly confident, assertive, and in control, he epitomized everything she secretly longed for but had been too ashamed to seek out after Preston's brutal rejection.

What she wanted from Jax as a lover was the opposite of the fight he wanted from her in the ring. The incongruity of his demands with her innate desires was tearing her apart. How would she get through the next few weeks of training? She couldn't. Not without taking drastic steps to solve the problem.

Chapter Five

"ANYTHING YOU WANT to discuss about our session yesterday?"

Arms folded and legs apart, Jax stood in the center of the training mat. His tight green and white fight shorts only served to inflame Marcy's already heightened state of arousal. Why couldn't he have worn baggy, torn shorts like some of other fighters, maybe an unwashed T-shirt, or better yet, a ski suit? Why did he have to taunt her with his chiseled pecs and toned abs when she was already at the edge of her rope? Damn Val and her insistence that a quick roll in the sheets was the solution. If Val hadn't kept on about it all afternoon, putting all the wrong images in Marcy's head, she would have had no problem keeping it professional.

None.

Really.

Jax frowned when she didn't respond. "You seem distracted. Were you okay last night?"

Marcy sucked in a sharp breath, and her cheeks heated as she thought about just how okay she had been after their session last night—the first night in over a year that she'd let anyone touch her in a way that wasn't entirely fight-related.

"Sure."

Jax outlined his strategy for their evening training session and the weeks to come. Marcy took a deep breath and forced herself to focus. She just had to get through the next hour and then … what? Tell him it wouldn't work or invite him home? Tell him it would work and invite him home? Just invite him home? She gritted her teeth. How about ripping off his clothes and running her hands over his muscular body?

"If you're happy with that," Jax said, wrapping up the outline, the end of which she'd missed in favor of indulging herself in torrid fantasies of her and Jax rolling around on the mats, "we'll start with some simple arm bars and triangles."

Relieved to be spared another session of his hands touching her body, Marcy dropped to her knees on the mat and waited for him to position himself on his back.

"Mount." He beckoned her forward, his voice curiously husky, and for a moment, she wondered if his touching exercise the other day had affected him as much as her. She crawled up his body and then sat astride his abdomen in full mount. God, his stomach was rock-hard. Just like the rest of him.

His body stiffened beneath her. "Christ, Marcy. Are you trying to kill me?"

Puzzled, she shrugged. "I thought you wanted me like this."

"I do. No. Fuck. I mean, to practice the submission, you need to be in high mount."

Understanding dawned, and she tried and failed to repress a smile. "Am I mounted too low for you, Jax?" She was sorely tempted to give a little wiggle because she could feel something hard pressing into her ass, and she was desperate to know if he was wearing a cup. In all her years of training, she'd never affected a guy this way, and she had to bite back a laugh.

His eyes blazed with liquid heat, and his voice dropped to a husky bark. "Move up."

Marcy eased herself up, her thighs parting wider as she positioned herself high on his chest, her knees under his armpits. "High mount is easier with female fighters," she said. "Your chest is so broad—"

He cut her off with a low growl. When she glanced down to see what she'd done to irritate him this time, she was caught in the blistering heat of his gaze.

"I'm on to you, little fighter." His eyes glinted, amused. "Don't think for a minute you'll distract me from doing what I came here to do."

A smile curled her lips. All week, she'd had to listen to the fighters at the gym talking about the aura of mystique surrounding Jax and his "fighter whisperer" ways. And yet his visible discomfort at her position on top of him made him seem all too human.

"Wouldn't dream of it."

He raised an eyebrow and exhaled through gritted teeth. "How about we try for mid guard?" The warmth of his breath caressed her inner thighs, and moisture flooded her sex. How unprofessional. She'd practiced this position countless times with other fighters in the club. Not once had she ever become so utterly and desperately aroused.

"Actually, probably better if we move to full guard." Jax bucked, throwing Marcy forward and onto her hands and knees, a standard defense to high guard but one that put her breasts within an inch of his lips.

Her nipples tightened, and she quickly rolled off him to hide her body's response. With gentle pressure, Jax pushed her to her back, then moved into a dominant position on top of her, taking his weight on his elbows, his legs tucked between hers.

So hot. So heavy. So utterly male. Desire coursed through her veins, and she tried to think of anything but the erotic weight of Jax on top of her.

Coach. Training. Professional. But her body, now a live wire, wasn't on board.

"How do you want me?" Her breathy voice shaded into a whisper of desire.

For a long moment, he didn't move. She could feel his heart drumming in his chest, hear the rasp of his breathing, and when she looked up at him, the heat in his eyes made her shudder.

He dropped his body, his hips pressing against the juncture of her thighs, his lips only inches away. Her pussy throbbed, and she arched under him. If she stretched up just the tiniest bit, she could have a little lick of his enticing, full lips. Just as she had imagined last night and every night since the day they'd met.

Kiss me. Kiss me. Kiss me.

As if he had heard her unspoken demand, he dropped his head, and his lips brushed over hers. Firm but fleeting, his kiss was there, and then it wasn't.

Fire streaked through Marcy's body with such intensity she forgot to breathe, burning its way straight to her core. She blinked and Jax was gone.

Alone, limp on the mat, she drew in a ragged breath. What the hell had she been thinking? Had she learned nothing from her breakup with Preston? Just because Jax was dominant in the ring didn't mean he was dominant in the bedroom. Or that he had any interest in her besides being a coach. Yet the more she was with him, the more she craved his touch—like a drug addict who had found the source of an endless fix.

It could only end in disaster.

◊ ◊ ◊

Christ.

Jax scrubbed his hand over his forehead in the back alley outside the gym. What the fucking hell had he done? He had always maintained a rigid line between the personal and professional aspects of his life. And what about the control he had fought so hard to achieve? Had he learned nothing from the deaths of his mother and sister? He had promised himself he would never feel that helpless again, and yet the minute Marcy walked into the gym, all he could think about was stripping off her clothes and getting her beneath him.

No doubt, she'd complain to Reid. And well she should. He'd taken advantage of his position and the physical proximity fight coaching required. But when he'd felt her soften beneath him, her breath soft and sweet on his cheek, he'd lost any semblance of control. Only the sight of Two Step, watching them from the cross trainer, had brought him to his senses long enough to get away.

Run away.

Just like he'd been doing for the last ten years.

The back door opened and closed, and Two Step joined him in the alley. For an awkward moment, neither of them spoke, and then Two Step leaned against the brick wall and sighed. "Gets hot in there."

Tension curled between them, born of an understanding only two men with an interest in the same woman could share. "Yeah."

"So you done for the night?" Two Step folded his arms, his massive biceps shimmering with sweat. Although Two Step didn't move away from the wall, Jax understood the underlying threat. He wasn't afraid of Two Step. Even after leaving the professional circuit, he'd kept up his training regime to stay in shape, focused, and better able to help the fighters with new techniques. Still, he wasn't interested in getting involved in a physical altercation, and Two Step's body language suggested he was spoiling for a fight.

"I've got Susie at eight and Davy at nine."

"But nothin' for the next forty-five minutes."

Jax raised an eyebrow at the unspoken admonishment. "You got something to say?"

"You hurt her and I'll come down on you so hard you won't know what hit you." Two Step's voice was soft and all the more menacing for it.

"I'm not here to hurt her. I'm here to help." He met Two Step's gaze. Marcy was lucky to have friends who cared about her so much. Always on the road, Jax didn't have time for friendships, and the constant relocation helped him avoid putting down roots. Roots meant relationships, and relationships meant pain.

"Good to hear. Hope it stays that way." Two Step let out a relieved breath. "So, you coming to the barbeque tonight? We're taking advantage of the downtime between events. Marcy will be there."

Jax frowned. "I thought you just warned me to stay away from her."

"I warned you not to hurt her. Couldn't go through that again. She was with this guy..." He swallowed hard. "She didn't show up at practice for a coupla days and didn't answer her phone, so I went to her place to see if she was okay. Bastard had hurt her bad. There were bruises on her wrists and ankles and ... fuck ... the marks on her back and the backs of her legs..." He scraped a hand over his head. "I was gonna go after him, but she told me he was gone and wouldn't be back. She wouldn't go to the police. Said she'd consented, but who'd consent to something like that?"

Someone with a kink or an interest in BDSM. A submissive. Just like he'd thought.

"All sorts of people with all sorts of interests out there." Jax understood better than most the prejudices faced by the kink community. He'd been ostracized by his family when he'd been open about his involvement with a local BDSM club. As a result, he'd lost valuable years with his mother and sister. Years he would never get back.

Two Step pushed away from the wall and headed for the door. "So, you coming?"

"Given the nature of my work, I don't usually socialize with my fighters. But thanks."

"Address is posted on the bulletin board in case you change your mind." Two Step pulled open the door, and the scent of lemon cleaner and stale sweat from the gym drifted into the alley. "We're a family here. We don't exclude people no matter how they want to fuck with our heads."

Jax laughed. "Not really what I do, but thanks."

Two Step paused and looked over his shoulder, his lips curled in an amused smile. "She likes whiskey. Straight up. No girly drinks for our Marcy. There's a good place round the corner … just in case you feel like picking up a bottle."

✧ ✧ ✧

"You're cut off, baby girl."

Marcy glared when Two Step snatched the shot glass out of her hand. "What the hell? I'm a grown woman. I know when I've had too much, and I'm not even close. I can still stand."

"You gotta eat something before I give it back." He gestured to a short Australian fighter with a surfer-dude twang flipping burgers on the grill. "Porter will set you up. He bought out Costco's meat department to make up for the lack of buns. You get something in your stomach, and then you can drink all you want."

"If you don't give me back that drink, you'll be getting something in your stomach, and it won't be food." Hands on her hips, she took what she hoped was a menacing step forward.

Two Step laughed, but his smile faded when Val handed her another glass.

"Her hand was empty," Val said with a shrug. "This is a party."

As if on cue, someone turned up the music, and Christina Aguilera's "Fighter" blasted through the speakers.

"Christ." Two Step spun away with a speed that belied his heavy frame, shouting as he stalked toward the sound system. "Who's responsible for the noise pollution? Where's my metal?"

"Thanks." Marcy clinked glasses with Val. "Sometimes he gets a tad overprotective." She'd never told Val what Two Step had seen that day he'd come to check on her after Preston left, although Val was pretty open-minded. Some secrets were better left buried.

They spent an hour catching up with the fighters. Tara and Lou had become a couple. Silvia and Stan had broken up. A few of the guys had new jobs, and some had been laid off. The Jackal was getting a divorce and wanted to know good pickup places. Val suggested he come by the sporting goods shop and hang out in aisle six, where she'd seen a couple making out beneath the cups. Marcy jabbed her in the side with her elbow, but Val was laughing too hard to care.

When the sun went down, Two Step turned on the outdoor lights and set up a makeshift fight ring. He offered a bottle of his best bourbon to anyone who could take him down. No takers. Two bottles?

"Make it whiskey and I'm in."

Marcy sucked in a sharp breath at the sound of Jax's voice, then stiffened when he came up behind her and put a hand on her shoulder.

"I heard it's your favorite drink." His voice was a low murmur in her ear, sending ripples of pleasure down her spine.

"You're going to fight Two Step?" Marcy shot him an incredulous glance over her shoulder. He was so close she could feel the heat from his body, smell the intoxicating scent of his cologne.

"No one else wants to do it."

"Doesn't that tell you something?" She had to fight the urge to brush her lips over his cheek. "They're fighters. They see Two Step every day, and they won't get in the ring with him."

"Tells me if I want to win, I'd better get moving." His hand slid down her arm, warm on her cool skin, and he gave her elbow a squeeze before joining Two Step in the makeshift ring.

"Oh. My. God." Val fanned herself with her hand. "That was seriously hot. He is so into you. Lookit him over there getting all ready to do the primal male thing and prove himself to you. Too bad it's gonna be so painful to watch. Two Step will crush him like a bug."

Marcy was looking. In fact, she couldn't look away. She'd thought he'd decided the training wasn't going to work after he'd cut their practice short earlier this evening. Maybe he'd had a change of heart.

Her pulse kicked up a notch when Jax and Two Step stripped off their shirts. God, he was breathtaking, all taut pecs and a six-pack for real. Although they wouldn't be doing many moves in their jeans. She indulged herself for a moment, imagining stripping off his jeans, sliding her hands over that tight ass, sinking to her knees, and taking him in her mouth.

"Uh … hello." Val jabbed her in the side. "You keep looking at him like that and he's gonna think you want to eat him up."

"I do."

What the fuck was he doing?

Jax leaned forward, hands on his knees, drawing in a deep breath. When he'd been fighting full time, he'd been a middleweight, at least eighty pounds lighter than Two Step. And although he'd stayed in shape and kept up his skills, he was no match for a heavier fighter in his prime. Already every part of his body ached, and he doubted he'd make it out of bed in the morning if he even made it out of the ring. And they'd only been fighting for a few minutes. But when he'd walked into the yard and spotted Marcy in that little black dress, her hair fanned out across her back, Two Step calling out his challenge, something in him had snapped. He wanted to show her he wasn't just a coach. He was a fighter, too.

"Tapping out?" Arms folded, Two Step grinned from the corner of the ring.

Bastard wasn't even winded.

Jax mustered all the bravado he could, given the screaming pain in his ribs. "Giving you time to come to your senses."

Two Step chuckled. "I got nothing to

prove." He looked over Jax's shoulder at Marcy, standing at the edge of the ring. "You do."

He straightened, biting back the flush of humiliation at being so easily read. "That's not—"

"Looks like you're ready to keep going." Two Step lunged forward, sweeping Jax's leg from under him. He hit the grass and rolled before Two Step could get his back, then jumped to his feet. Unbelievably, Two Step was wide open. Jax hit him with a right cross followed by a left hook, and Two Step went down hard.

"Fuck." Jax bent down beside him. "What's going on? I didn't hit you that hard."

Two Step tapped the grass, indicating he was conceding the fight to Jax, then rubbed his jaw. "You owe me, brother. Big-time."

"You threw the fight for me?" He helped Two Step to his feet as the fighters around them cheered.

Two Step's gaze flicked to Marcy and then back to Jax. "Not for you. For my baby girl. Told you. We're a family here. We look out for each other. Can't have her thinking she's hooking up with a guy who can't hold his own in a fight."

"We're not—"

"You'd better be." Two Step's eyes narrowed as Marcy joined them in the ring. "Or else you owe me a fight."

Jax thought she'd go to Two Step first. After all, he'd supposedly taken two hits that had knocked him to the ground. But it was Jax she spoke to first.

"Congratulations. No one's ever taken Two Step down." She traced a finger over his bicep, and all his blood rushed to his groin.

"For a while there, I thought you were in trouble." Her finger lingered on his skin, and with adrenaline still coursing through his veins after the fight, it was everything he could do to keep his hands by his sides. "I thought you were … just a coach."

He didn't want to lie. "Marcy, I…"

Two Step cleared his throat and drew a warning finger across his neck, mafia-style, drawing Marcy's attention.

"You okay?" She raised an eyebrow.

"All good. Just didn't see that one coming."

"Indeed."

Jax shot Two Step a questioning look. He couldn't tell if Marcy knew or not, and if she did, what she thought of Two Step's performance. She was very difficult to read. But then, so was he.

Two Step just shrugged and gestured at the makeshift bar on a picnic table in the corner. "Your prize is over there. Make sure she eats between shots, otherwise she gets a bit crazy."

"Two Step!"

He widened his eyes in mock surprise at her outburst. "What? Have you forgotten the beach barbeque last year when you decided to go swimming naked outta bounds? Or the time you decided to drag race with Susie down that country lane behind Stan's place? Or how 'bout that time you told the cops—"

"Enough." She blushed and pressed her lips together. Jax's stomach tightened. He wanted to be the one to put that flush in her cheeks, and now that he suspected they might share a kink, he could think of a dozen ways to put it there, none of them involving words.

"Sounds like you lead an exciting life." Jax pressed a hand against her lower back and led her toward the picnic table. Despite his best intentions, he couldn't help curling his fingers into the curve of her narrow waist. His cock stiffened, and he dropped his hand. Fuck. Maybe showing up tonight wasn't such a good idea.

"Authority issues." She laughed lightly and chatted with a fighter at the bar who procured the promised bottles, one for each of them, giving Jax a wink after Marcy had turned away.

"Name's Lou. Heard about you coming to help us out. Good fight … I think."

Jax gritted his teeth. "I didn't really…"

Lou cut him off with a laugh. "It's how we do things here. We got each other's backs. You've been at lots of clubs. I'm sure it's the same."

"Actually, it isn't," Jax said. "A lot of clubs I've worked at have been highly competitive, everyone looking out for themselves, because ultimately it's one person and not the team in the ring. But this club"—he looked around at the crowd spread across every inch of Two Step's lawn—"is a real team. This kind of support can make the difference between a mediocre fighter and a great one."

"Family." Lou smiled. "We're a family. Not just a team."

Jax nodded. Excelsior was the kind of club he had trained in when he had first started fighting: small enough to be supportive, but big enough to attract good quality fighters and coaches. His disenchantment with the fight world had started only after he'd joined a larger, more competitive club. Now, as he looked around at the Excelsior "family," he wondered if that kind of support would have made a difference, not only when he'd lost his mother and sister, but also when he'd suffered the knock-out punch that ended his career.

"Hey, you okay?" Marcy slipped her hand around his arm, and his moment of melancholy dissolved in a rush of heat that shot straight to his groin.

"Yeah." He nodded at the open bottle in her

hand. “Drinking it straight, I see. No glass for you.”

Marcy laughed and his chest tightened. “I was about to pour when I saw you with Lou. You looked kinda lost in thought for a second.”

He raised an eyebrow to hide his discomfort at being caught out. “I was wondering what was taking you so long with the drinks.”

Warm and throaty, her laugh did strange things to his stomach. He reached out and tucked a wayward strand of hair behind her ear, his fingers lingering on the soft curve of her jaw, and in that moment, something changed in the air between them. Marcy’s eyes darkened, and she licked her lips, that lovely blush spreading across her cheeks.

“You want to take this bottle to my place?”

Jax didn’t even try to dissemble. Didn’t waste a moment wondering if this was the right thing to do. If the looks they were getting from Marcy’s teammates were anything to go by, he already had the Club Excelsior stamp of approval.

“Yes.”

Chapter Six

HIS ARMS WERE around her before she had even closed the front door.

Pulling her into his body, Jax groaned and covered her lips with his. Hot and hungry, his tongue swept into her mouth, leaving no inch untouched, a promise of what was to come.

"Jax. Wait." She tried to pull away. "Let me close the door."

Without releasing her, he shifted position, backing her against the door, stopping only when it closed with a loud bang.

Marcy grimaced. "The neighbors aren't going to like that."

"They're not going to like listening to you scream with pleasure, either." Jax nuzzled her neck. “And that’s what’s going to happen next.”

“Someone is overly confident in his abilities.” She fought to repress a smile as she met his half-lidded gaze.

“Realistic.”

Marcy melted. She’d never been with a man as confident as Jax. Or as sexual. Everything about him, from the way he moved his body to the husky timbre of his voice, to the firm, unyielding press of his lips, suggested he wasn’t lying. And, oh god, she was dying to find out if that was true.

Her words came out in a whisper. “Show me.”

But his hands were already at her hips, tugging up her dress as he deepened the kiss. Almost frantic with need, Marcy yanked open his belt and worked the buttons of his fly, her fingers trembling with an urgency she didn’t understand. Sure, it had been a while since she’d been with a guy, but she wasn’t desperate. And it wasn’t like he was about to cut and run like Preston. He didn’t know anything about her secret desires, and he never would.

"Fuck." Jax slammed her against the door and slid his fingers along the edge of her panties. "You got any sentimental attachment to these?"

"No." She brushed her lips over the stubble on his jaw, shuddering at the tiny burst of pain.

Jax tore her panties away with one firm tug, and her breath caught in her throat. Even when Preston had agreed to give her kink a try for one night, sex had never been like this. Raw, wild, uninhibited. She had a feeling if she growled and bit Jax, he would bite her back. Her mouth watered at the thought, and for a moment, the words danced on the tip of her tongue. *Bite me. Hurt me. Spank me. Whip me.* But years of suppressing her desires made her hold them back.

Swallowing hard, she shoved his jeans down his thighs, then freed his erection from his boxers. His cock, thick and hard, bounced in her direction, and she wrapped her fingers around him and squeezed. Jax groaned and covered her hand with his own, tightening her fingers around his shaft.

"Condom. Back pocket."

With her free hand, Marcy reached around

and found the condom. "Convenient."

"I aim to please."

She gave him one last hard stroke, then released him to open the condom. "And please you do."

He threaded his hand through her hair, tightening his grip as she rolled the condom over his erection. A burst of pleasure-pain shot straight to her clit, and she bit back a moan. He seemed to know what she liked without her telling him. Maybe he would see into the darkest recesses of her heart and make her dreams come true.

She'd only just finished unrolling the condom when Jax cupped her ass and lifted her against his hips, bracing her against the wall as he commenced a full-on assault with his mouth. Forehead, cheeks, nose, chin, and lips. Nothing was left untouched. His hand cupped her breast, squeezing through the cotton of her dress, his thumb gliding back and forth until her nipple peaked beneath her bra. She wanted his hands on her skin, his lips and teeth on her nipple, but with the zipper at her back and his cock prodding at her entrance, she wasn't prepared to wait.

"I want you inside me. Now." With her arms around his neck, she levered herself up. Jax pulled back and slid one hand between her thighs and over the curve of her sex.

"Who's in charge?"

Who's in charge? Did he know how long she'd yearned to hear those words? To have someone who knew what he was doing take control? To give herself over in trust? Was Jax the kind of man who could dominate in bed, or was he just playing around?

Swallowing hard, she said, "You."

He gave a satisfied grunt and pressed his lips against her ear. "Yes, that's right. Me. You do what I say when I say, and you get only what I want to give."

Marcy shuddered, and her pussy slicked with heat at his tone: firm, commanding, unyielding. No, Jax wasn't playing around, and she held her breath, waiting for more.

"Are you ready for me?" He stroked along her soaked folds, then pressed one finger deep inside her. A low guttural groan was the only answer she could give as he withdrew.

"Good girl." Jax's fingers curled into her ass, and he lifted her, then slammed her down hard over his cock.

Marcy gasped. Oh god. So big. So thick. His shaft pressed against her inner walls, and she felt at once unbearably stretched and deliciously full. But before she could adjust to his size, he lifted her and slammed her down again. This time, it was all pleasure. So much pleasure moisture flooded her sex, and she tightened around him.

"Fuck, yes." He lifted her again, sliding her up against the cool wood surface, the head of his cock teasing her entrance. And then he thrust in deep and hard, yanking her down until he was in so deep the tip of his cock hit her cervix. Marcy clutched at his shoulders and moaned.

"Take it." His voice dropped to a husky growl as he lifted her and pulled her down again. "Open for me and take it all until there isn't an inch of your pussy I haven't touched. I want you, Marcy. I want you to be utterly and completely mine."

And then he was hammering into her, using

her momentum and the thrust of her hips to drive deeper, thrust harder, sending her desire spiraling out of control.

"Don't stop, Jax. Don't stop."

He stopped, his cock buried deep inside her, his chest heaving, slicked in sweat. "Who's in charge?"

She panted the words, the ache in her pussy overshadowing her fear that what was so arousing to her was only a game to him. "You are."

"That means I decide if we stop."

She gritted her teeth and nodded. If he didn't move in the next thirty seconds, she was going to kill him.

"Say it." His quiet command sent her pulse racing.

"You decide if we stop."

He studied her for a long moment, then pulled out in one long, slow movement, until the head of his cock rested just inside her slit, enough to tease but not enough to satisfy. A whine escaped her lips, and she rocked against him.

"Shhh, I'll take care of you." Bracing her

against the wall, he slid one hand between them and spread her moisture up and around her clit, his thumb circling closer and closer but never touching where she needed it most. When every muscle in her body had tightened, her need to climax so great she was prepared to beg, he thrust into her hard and fast, then pinched her clit between his thumb and forefinger, sending her tumbling over the edge before she could catch her breath.

Marcy screamed into his shoulder as pleasure crashed through her in thunderous waves, rippling out to her fingers and toes, fuzzing her brain until she tasted the tang of blood and realized she'd bitten him.

But if he noticed, he gave no sign. Instead, he pounded into her, drawing out the last waves of her orgasm. Jax stiffened inside her and came with a shout, his fingers digging into her ass.

Heart thudding, Marcy sagged against Jax's chest and inhaled the scents of sweat and sex and the sharp, fresh tang of his cologne. If this was the only time, she wanted to remember everything. Every touch. Every taste. Every sound. Every scent. And the sheer blissful feeling of letting someone else take control.

He stroked her hair, his cheek pressed against her temple, the gentle gesture making her chest tighten with emotion. Jax was only here for a few weeks, and then he'd be gone. Her best-case scenario. No ties. No lies. No attachments. No risk of wanting to share that secret side of herself and the concomitant rejection that would follow. And yet, a sliver of longing had worked its way into her heart.

She sighed and leaned into his touch, wondering why their brief encounter was causing her so much angst. She'd had one-night stands before and walked away in the morning without any regrets.

Damn.

He could feel her pulling away, her emotional withdrawal evident in the stiffening of her body and the clench of her fist against his chest. Given the nature of their professional relationship, he'd come on too strong, but what the hell was he supposed to do when she'd made it clear what she wanted from him? He'd been holding on to his control by the thinnest of threads, but the moment she'd yanked open his belt, he was gone.

And as for getting her out of his system, he already knew one time wouldn't be enough. But something was wrong with his little fighter, and he wasn't going to find out what it was standing in the hallway at half-mast.

Jax excused himself to dispose of the condom and grabbed his clothes on his way to the bathroom. Yeah, he wanted her again, but if he didn't heed the warning in her silence, it would be over before it began.

When he returned, Marcy was curled up on the couch, her tank top and pajama pants a message he couldn't ignore. Still, he wasn't a man easily put off. He settled beside her, throwing his arm over the back of the couch and tucking her against him, her head resting on his chest.

"You've never been so quiet." He stroked a finger along her arm, delighted when goose bumps rose on her skin. So, she wasn't unaffected by him, after all.

"I've never been so confused." She softened against his chest, and Jax let out a breath. Okay, he hadn't totally screwed it up.

"What's confusing?"

"This." She looked up at him, her eyes clouded with emotion. "We shouldn't have done this. How will I train with you now? I've got a big event coming up, and there isn't enough time for Reid to hire someone new."

Jax bristled. "You don't need someone new. I can still work with you—"

"It changes everything." She scrubbed her hand over her face and gave him a half smile. "All I'll be able to think about if you're mounting me or putting me into submission is sex."

"That's pretty much all I thought about before," he said, hoping his honesty would ease her tension.

Marcy gave a light laugh. "Same."

He pressed a kiss to her forehead. "Then nothing changes. We'll still work together to help you reach your goal."

But how? Although dominant in the ring, Marcy was submissive in the bedroom, and he suspected that aspect of her personality was holding her back. For some reason, in the ring, her mind sent a signal to submit instead of fight, just enough to freeze her at a critical moment as her conscious awareness tried to push it away.

Jax sighed. She'd responded beautifully to his commands. How could he train her to fight submission when she so readily embraced it? He had to ensure she could maintain a barrier between personal and professional.

Not easy to do with Jax straddling the line.

Two days after her encounter with Jax, Marcy pushed open the door to Reid's office and frowned. "So, what's so important that you have to drag my sorry ass in here just as I was about to go home and sink into a nice hot bath?"

She tossed her gym bag on the floor and threw herself into the chair across from Reid's desk, annoyed at being summoned before she could escape the gym after successfully avoiding talking to Jax about anything except training for the last two days. And yet, the memory of their heated encounter lingered, teased and taunted her senses. Distracting.

Reid shoved a piece of paper across his desk. "I've just received the new rules about the state championship. For a shot at your weight title, you need to be in the top four fighters in Washington State. If you're in the top eight, you have a chance as an alternate. You're number ten. They make their decision in six weeks, so if you want a secure place, you'll need to improve your ranking."

Marcy sucked in a sharp breath and leaned forward in her seat. "Have you heard from that new promotion, ROC, about the fight in two weeks? I could boost my ranking with a win at that event if they pick me."

"They picked you. I just heard from them today."

"That's great." A smile creased her face. "And perfect timing. A win will kick me up to number eight and…" Her breath hitched when Reid frowned. "Why the long face?"

He scraped his hand through his hair and leaned back in his chair. "Jax doesn't think you'll be ready."

She looked at him, aghast. "Not ready? I've been training for this kind of opportunity all year. Until the last fight, I was four and oh, and that fight doesn't count on the circuit because it was just for show. I'm ready. My issue will be sorted well before the event."

Reid gave an uncomfortable shrug. "He doesn't think so."

Marcy's blood chilled. Why had Jax told Reid there was a problem before discussing it with her? And what the hell was he thinking getting in the way of her dreams? Why had he been with her the other night? Did he know about the upcoming event? Did he feel sorry for her? Was it a pity fuck?

"You're my coach," she said, her voice uncharacteristically sharp. "Not him. You signed me up for that event before he even came to Excelsior. If you thought I was ready then, I'm more than ready now."

A pained expression crossed Reid's face.

"You'd never been knocked out before I signed you up. You'd frozen before but never when it was a life-or-death situation. I don't have the skills to deal with that kind of problem. Jax does. So I have to listen his advice, and his advice is not to put you in the ring."

Her hands tightened on the armrests of the chair until her knuckles whitened. "You can't pull me from the event now. My name is on the card. And I want to fight, Reid. I'll fight and I'll win and I'll get a place on the list."

"Jax thinks it would be a mistake, and I agree." He leaned back in his chair. "You're number ten. The state championships are a few months away. Plenty of time to deal with the problem, and maybe by then a few people will have dropped off the list."

"That's not a risk I'm willing to take." She didn't wait for his response. Even if they weren't done, she couldn't stay there another minute. Jax had some explaining to do.

"Marcy."

She paused on her way out and looked back over her shoulder, smoothing her face into an expressionless mask.

Reid's throat tightened as he swallowed. "I'm sorry. I thought he'd talked to you about it."

Not trusting herself to speak, she walked away.

Chapter Seven

"BASTARD!"

Jax grabbed a towel and wiped himself down as Marcy stalked across the mats, her shout echoing in the near-empty gym. Eyes glittering fever-bright, jaw tense, body trembling, she was breathtaking in her fury.

Don't go there. Their nightly training sessions had become one erotic torture after the next. Rolling across the mat with Marcy's sweet body tucked against him, wrapping himself around her and coaxing her to fight submission without giving in to his base desires had introduced a whole new level of hell for his self-control. He should never have let things go as far as they had. Talk about a major fucking disaster.

She pulled up short in front of him and drew in a ragged breath, her fists clenching and unclenching by her sides. Jax's skin prickled. Except for the brief time they'd been intimate, he'd never seen Marcy anything but calm and controlled and maybe just a bit flustered. This was a different Marcy. Marcy in full armor.

"You told him I wasn't ready," she spat out. "If I don't fight in the ROC event, I won't have a shot at the state championship."

His stomach tightened. Damn Reid. Their conversation was meant to be confidential, at least until he'd had a discussion with Marcy. But Reid was up against a deadline and hadn't given him a choice.

Still, it didn't change the facts, and he had never been one to dance around an issue.

"I'm sorry, but I couldn't lie to him. And he's worried you'll wind up in the hospital again. He didn't want to risk your safety." Neither did he, especially not now.

Her nostrils flared. "You're supposed to tell *me* first. Let *me* explain or fix things. Update *me* on my progress. I could have worked harder, trained more…"

He held up his hands, palms forward. "It doesn't work like that, Marcy. There's nothing else you could do. It's a process."

"A process." Bitterness tinged her words. "That's what our training has been? A process?"

The pain in her voice sliced through him with the accuracy of a surgeon's blade. He knew exactly what she was saying. He could read between the lines. But he couldn't give her the reassurance she so obviously needed. And he didn't want to raise the concern that was keeping him up every night. He didn't want to destroy her dreams, especially if he wasn't one hundred percent certain he was right.

"Yes. It doesn't happen at once."

She bristled. "What about the other night? What was that? Did you fuck me because you felt guilty? Or out of pity because I'll have to train another full year for a shot at the title? Was that your twisted way of saying sorry?"

His stomach clenched at the pain and anger in her voice. "I didn't go looking for you the other night thinking things would turn out as they did. But you were already under my skin. I couldn't stop thinking about you. And when I saw what you'd been hiding from me, it was too much. You're impossible to resist. I wanted more of you than I get in the fight ring. I want the softness under your armor, too."

"I hate you." Her voice rose in pitch, drowning out his words. "I knew I didn't need a coach. Especially someone who would mess up my career. If it weren't for you, I would be on that card with the full support of Reid and the team. Now I have to fight knowing he doesn't think I'm ready to be there." She turned away, and he reached out and clasped her shoulder, spinning her to face him.

"Wait."

"Don't. Touch. Me." She wrenched herself away, and then, as if a dam broke, she hit his chest, one frenzied blow after another until he grabbed her wrists and pinned them behind her back.

"Stop, Marcy. I don't want to hurt you. What happened at the Tri-Star event would've happened even if I hadn't been here. Reid had doubts about you before, and has the same doubts now."

Chest heaving, chin quivering, eyes glistening with tears, she met his gaze. "Too late. You already hurt me."

He only meant to kiss the tear away. But as his lips glided over her cheek, she turned into him and pressed her lips to his, so soft and sweet he ached with pleasure. Before she could back away, he cupped her head with his hand, holding her still, and kissed her with infinite tenderness, showing her in his gesture what she refused to hear in his words.

"Don't." Breaking their kiss, she choked back a sob and leaned her forehead against his chest. "I told Reid I was going to fight anyway. I want it so much. I've worked so hard. I'm not about to let it slip away for something so intangible I'm not even sure it's real."

He released her wrists and wrapped his arms around her, resting his chin on her head. "I was going to talk to you, but Reid put me on the spot, and I can't recommend putting a fighter in the ring if she isn't physically or mentally ready.

Especially because that's what happened to me, and I know how bad it can be. One month after my sister died, I went into the ring. I was still an emotional wreck, and I thought I heard her voice in the crowd. Lost focus. Got knocked out so bad I was unconscious almost a week. That's when I decided to give it up and help people instead."

Her bottom lip quivered, and her body softened. "I'm sorry about what happened to you, but you're wrong about me."

"I was wrong about many things, but not this. The flyweights on ROC's card are all submission experts. You're not ready for them yet."

Not now. Maybe not ever. And definitely not with him as her coach. He couldn't deny that something about her called out to his dominant side, drawing him in like a beacon. And yet, in the ring, he needed to teach her to fight, not submit. He'd never faced such a struggle with the professional-personal divide.

She stiffened in his arms, and for a moment, he thought—feared—she would pull away.

Instead, she sagged against him. "Now what?"

For him, quitting was the obvious solution, but the problem was deeper than that. Aside from dealing with his deep attraction to her, he felt compelled to tell Marcy the truth. She would need to know that, unless she could somehow maintain the divide between personal and professional, she might not have what it took to become a championship fighter. Sometimes sexual needs bled out into the real world. For most people, it wasn't a problem. For Marcy, it could kill her career.

And the truth would kill her dreams.

With impeccable timing, Reid stepped into the gym, his gaze flicking from Jax to Marcy and back to Jax. With a resigned shake of his head, he tossed Marcy the keys.

"I'm heading out. Everyone else is gone. Lock up for me and then slide the keys through the mail slot. I have another set at home."

Jax waited until the door closed behind Reid before he spoke again, seeking a way to put some distance between them, regain perspective … control. Maybe even discover he was wrong. "Show me it doesn't happen all the time."

"Damn right I will." Marcy kicked off her shoes and stalked through the gym toward the mats. Jax followed behind, admiring the way her jeans hugged her lush ass like a second skin. Despite the emotionally volatile situation, he couldn't help his body's response when she turned and he caught sight of the tiny tank top stretched tight over her generous breasts.

His gut tightened as he took his position on his back on the floor. Marcy straddled his chest and leaned over him, her thighs warm against his rib cage. He drew in a deep breath and caught a light floral scent that made his balls tighten. Perfume. He'd never thought she'd be a perfume kind of girl.

"Do it, Jax. Do it now."

God, he wanted to do it.

Swallowing hard, he pulled her into the submission, his leg over her shoulder, her throat bared to the pressure of his shin. She struggled for a few seconds until he tightened the hold, and then her body stiffened, and she sucked in a sharp breath.

"There," he said, his voice calm and even. "That will lose you the fight."

"No, Jax. I'm just … tense. It's hard to grapple in street clothes."

"It's not the clothes, it's you. Something is still holding you back." He released his grip and rolled to his side, propping his head up with his hand, trying to maintain enough of a distance to enable him to think clearly. She stretched out beside him, mirroring his position, and he stroked his thumb over her cheek. But instead of telling her what she needed to know, coward that he was, he said, "We'll keep working on it."

Her bottom lip quivered. "I'm going to fight in the ROC event, whether you can help me or not."

"I can do a lot in two weeks." Hell, he'd done a lot in one week. He had fallen too hard, too fast, and there was no going back. Throwing caution aside, he leaned in and brushed his lips over hers. "I can do a lot now," he whispered.

Liquid heat surged through Marcy's veins as Jax caught her mouth in a searing kiss. She hadn't come here for this. After Reid had given her the news, she'd intended to give Jax a piece of her mind, prove him wrong, and then walk away. Forever. But as he moved over her body, his heat surrounding her as he eased her onto her back, she couldn't deny she wanted him with an ache that burned into her soul.

"Fuck." He buried his face in her neck, his five o'clock shadow scraping over her skin as he slipped his hand beneath her and stroked the arch of her bare back. His lips slid down to the sensitive juncture between her neck and her shoulder, and he sucked hard until a tiny burst of pain made her gasp.

"More."

He bit down, gently at first, then increased the pressure until the pain made her eyes water and the pleasure sent a surge of moist heat between her legs. A moan ripped out of her chest. *God, it had been so long.*

Jax pushed himself up on his elbows and studied her face, considering. Then he eased her arms over her head, clasping her wrists with one hand. Her back arched with the strain, and she sucked in a sharp breath as arousal shot through her like white lightning.

His eyes widened, and then his voice dropped to a low, husky growl. "You like it rough, little fighter."

Memories came back. The soft thud of the flogger. The rattle of chains. Pain and pleasure. Preston's muttered apologies as he packed up his disgust and self-loathing and ran out the door.

No. Jax wasn't Preston, who'd had to be told what to do. He wasn't a man who had to be guided or led. For the last week, Jax had manipulated her body, coaxed her to do his will. She wanted that again. But not just in the ring. She wanted him to take her as far as she could go.

"Yes."

Corded neck tightening as he swallowed, he slanted his lips over hers and kissed her with a raw, animal need that took her breath away. "Marcy."

Her heart surged as he rasped her name, and then his lips were on her again, feathering kisses down her neck to the crescent of her breasts. He nipped the soft flesh straining above the vee of her tank top until she was panting beneath him.

"More. Jax ... please."

A deep growl erupted from his lips. "Need to see you this time. All of you." He released her wrists and stripped her with quick efficiency. No gentle slide of clothing. No slow reveal. No brush of fingers over her heated skin. Within moments, she was naked, stretched out on the soft vinyl mat, the cool air whispering over her body, bared for his pleasure.

His gaze raked over her, and then he exhaled a long, sensual breath. "So beautiful." He cupped her breasts in his warm hands and squeezed gently before dragging his thumbs over her nipples, circling them until they peaked.

Marcy's thoughts scattered. Fevered with desire, she arched into him, offering herself up for his pleasure. Jax bent down and captured her left nipple, grating his teeth back and forth.

"Oh, yes." She hissed out a breath.

With a wicked smile, he released her, chuckling when she moaned her displeasure.

"My little fighter's a bad girl." He abandoned her breasts for a slow, leisurely torture of her body, alternating between soft, warm kisses and small, sharp nips that left her gasping for air.

When he reached her mound, he paused and feathered his fingers lightly over her heated skin. "Bare."

Marcy swallowed past the lump in her throat. Some men didn't like their women bare. Her first serious boyfriend hadn't touched her for weeks after her first Brazilian, his lips curling in distaste when he saw what she'd done.

"It's easier when I'm fighting." She gave an apologetic shrug.

Jax smiled and pressed a kiss to her mound, his lips soft and warm on her skin. "Beautiful."

Then, as if he couldn't bear to be clothed, he pushed himself away, stripping off his jeans and his shirt with the same quick efficiency he had used to undress her before tossing them into a heap on the mat.

Although she had seen him wearing nothing but fight shorts, it wasn't until that moment that she was able to fully appreciate the raw beauty of his lean, muscular body—over six feet of sheer masculine power. Her gaze followed the ridges of muscle over his narrow hips to his cock, hot and heavy, jutting from a dark nest of curls, the thick head pink and swollen. A drop of moisture glistened at the tip. She licked her lips, imagining how he would taste.

"If you keep looking at me like that, I'll get ideas that'll result in a rapid end to this encounter."

A smile curled her lips. "Next time then."

Kneeling between her parted legs, he feathered kisses over her breasts and her abdomen, the gentle brush of his lips making her tremble with need. But when he skipped over the curve of her sex and nipped the sensitive skin of her inner thigh, she gritted her teeth in frustration. Threading her fingers through his hair, she tugged him up to where she wanted him to go.

"No." His deep, commanding tone froze her in an instant. She felt the rush of forbidden desire coiling deep in her belly, and a soft moan escaped her lips.

Jax sat up and studied her so intently she instinctively dropped her gaze. When she lifted her head again, the look he gave her, carnal, warning, seared her to the core.

"Hands over your head."

She complied without thinking, and he grasped her wrists, locking them together, tugging them higher until her body arched, offering her breasts up for his licking pleasure.

"I know what you need." He sucked and bit one nipple then the other as his free hand slid between her thighs to cup her sex, his warm palm pressing against her clit. She inhaled a ragged breath at his possessive touch.

"You want the freedom of submission, but you're afraid to give up control. If I had to guess, I'd say it's a need you buried, and it's resurfaced in the ring."

She shook her head as the feelings of shame she'd carried with her since Preston's abrupt departure washed over her, dimming her arousal. "I'm not submissive. I'm a fighter. Always have been. It's like you said … I just need it … rough."

"You need more than that."

Her thoughts shattered as his fingers slid through her folds, teasing her with the heat of his hand against her throbbing flesh.

"Some needs aren't meant to be denied." He thrust a thick finger deep inside her pussy, and her hips came off the mat.

"Yes." She whispered her confession, her voice thin and raw with desire and a filament of fear. Just like that, he'd ripped away the veil and peered into her soul. But instead of recoiling as Preston had done, he accepted … understood.

Tightening his grip on her wrists, he eased a second finger inside her, stretching her as he stroked against her sensitive inner walls. Marcy writhed around the exquisite intrusion. "Oh god."

With a strangled groan, he leaned over and brushed his lips over hers, then kissed her so thoroughly she was in no doubt he wanted her. Nor did she have any doubts about who was in control.

"If we knew each other better, I would restrain you more securely," he murmured. "Hands and feet. Spread open for me. Available for my pleasure. But that requires a certain level of trust, and we're not there yet."

A fierce wave of hunger washed over her, and she groaned. Although she ached to be fully restrained, he was right. Only a few hours ago, she hadn't trusted him at all.

"Jax." His name ripped from her throat in a pleading whimper.

"Don't worry, little fighter. I'll take care of you." He paused, studied her from beneath his lashes, his gaze focused, intent. "Have you played before, Marcy?"

"Yes," she said softly, incredulous she was having this conversation. "But not much, and my partners didn't know what they were doing. They didn't understand. I went to a fetish club once to learn the basics—safety, techniques—but I didn't want to play with anyone I didn't know."

"You know me. Do you want to play?" His thumb brushed over her clit, feather light, but enough to make her gasp. Her hips jerked off the floor.

"Hell, yes." She writhed under his touch,

aroused as much by the knowledge he understood her kink as by the sensations flooding her body.

"So close, aren't you?" He touched her cheek gently. "Let's take you higher."

Chapter Eight

"OVER YOU GO."

Without warning, Jax flipped Marcy to her stomach and then positioned her on all fours, cheek on the mat, ass in the air. Marcy shuddered as he smoothed his hand over her heated skin. Somehow he could see her deepest desires and was dragging them one by one into the light.

"Should I spank you, little fighter? Punish you for hitting me?"

Craving took hold of her, dark and delicious. She sensed his spanking would be nothing like Preston's pathetic raps on her ass. There would be no wrinkling of the nose or twitching of the lips. No murmured apologies and self-reproach. It would be painful, and it would be real.

"Yes."

He parted her legs with a thick thigh and pressed down on her lower back, holding her in place. "Did you learn about safe words at the club?"

Marcy forced the words through the lump in her throat. "Red for stop. Yellow to slow down. Green to go ahead."

"And now?"

"Green." Anticipation ratcheted through her, and shame melted into a need so intense it took her breath away.

"Have you ever been spanked before?" Jax rubbed deep circles over her ass, bringing the blood to the surface, warming her up. She knew how it was supposed to work, had guided a few adventurous boyfriends and Preston through every step. But Jax clearly didn't need instruction, and she trembled under his touch, desperate for that first smack—the blow that would tell her if he was everything she had imagined he would be.

"A few times, but it wasn't good. Not like how I thought. Like I said, they didn't know what they were doing."

Jax's hand tightened on her lower back. "Lucky for you, I do."

She froze at the first blow, although it was nothing more than a light slap, her body stiffening, her breath leaving in a rush. He gave her a moment to recover, and then he smacked her again. This time on the other cheek. An exquisite pain.

Yes, yes, yes. So good.

He set up a steady rhythm, alternating cheeks and quadrants, varying speed and intensity. The room echoed with the crack of his palm on her skin, the rasp of his breath, and her whimpers-turned-cries.

"Breathe," he murmured. "Use your safe word if you need me to stop." But he didn't slow down, didn't let up. Not that she wanted him to.

He smacked harder, and fire streaked across her skin. With each blow, pleasure and pain coalesced into an intoxicating cocktail of desire that sent her mind spinning and made her sex pulse and throb with need. A low, guttural groan ripped from her throat, unwanted, uncontrolled.

"That's it, baby. Let me hear you." He smacked her again and again and again until sensation flooded her brain and she was barely aware of where his hand ended or her body began.

"Easy." His deep voice rumbled in her ear, soft and smooth as Two Step's best bourbon, pulling her back before he slid his fingers through her soaked folds.

Marcy gasped and tried to jerk away from the unexpected intimate caress, but he held her firmly.

"You like being spanked, Marcy. You like submitting to my will." He trailed her wetness along her inner thigh and then released her with a sigh. "I would love to take you further, but not today."

As the fog cleared from her mind, she whimpered her displeasure, and Jax laughed. "Still don't think you're submissive? I'm not done with you yet, but if I don't take it slow, I might scare you away. You aren't the only one with hidden needs, and I don't think I'll last."

With the skill he used to manipulate her

body in the ring, he flipped her over, grasping her wrists with one hand, and tugging her arms up and over her head. He jerked her thighs apart and, without warning, plunged two fingers into her pussy, slick and swollen with need.

"Oh god." She tilted her hips and ground against him, pulling against his firm grip as her heels dug into the mat. His thumb pressed down on her clit, and pleasure became pain, driving her arousal higher.

"Oh. Oh. Jax."

And then his mouth, hot and wet, clamped over her nipple, and he bit down gently. His fingers surged deep, rubbing along her sensitive inner walls until she was bucking and jerking against him.

Too much. Too intense. Her body arced upward, tight as a bowstring as sensation reverberated through her, the lingering burn on her ass only fueling her desire.

"That's it," Jax murmured. "Let go, little fighter. Give it up. Yield to me."

He felt the moment she let go, groaned as she came apart in his hands.

Cock throbbing, he drew out her pleasure, stroking along her inner walls as her sex pulsed around him, her moisture trickling over his wrist. So fucking wet.

He'd never seen anything so arousing. Never wanted anything as badly as he wanted to be inside her. Ever.

Finally, she sighed and softened, quivered beneath him. Gently, he withdrew his fingers and scrambled to find his jeans. In a moment, he had retrieved the condom from his wallet and sheathed himself.

His gaze raked over her beautiful body as he knelt between her parted legs. Her arms were loose above her head, thighs soft, open. Her pussy, pink and swollen, glistened, beckoned.

She lifted heavy eyes to his and whispered, "I need you."

God, this woman was made for him. Naturally, beautifully submissive. A perfect match for his dominant nature.

"Please, Jax. Don't make me wait." She parted her creamy thighs, and his control shattered. Within a heartbeat, his cock was pressed against her slick entrance. She whimpered, tilting her hips, an invitation he couldn't refuse.

With a low, guttural groan, Jax moved over her, covering her with his body, and sank into her hot, wet channel. Marcy gasped and arched, pushing against him. *Christ.* He couldn't hold out. His hips bucked, and he thrust and withdrew, driving into her slick, moist heat over and over again. When he felt her pussy quiver and tighten, he slid his hand between them and pinched her clit. "Come for me, little fighter."

She climaxed with a shriek, her body shaking, trembling violently beneath him.

Too much. Too beautiful. "Fuck." He hammered into her, his cock thickening, engorging, until finally his spine tingled, and pleasure erupted from his body in long, hot, heated jerks.

He collapsed, his chest pressed tight against her breasts. When the fog began to lift from his brain, he pressed a soft kiss to her cheek, eliciting a tiny shudder from her body.

God. He wanted her all over again.

Fuck. What the hell had he done? He'd resolved this morning to keep it professional, and his resolve had lasted barely twelve hours.

He pulled away and disposed of the condom. When he returned, Marcy was curled up against the wall, a first aid blanket wrapped around her. Her hair had come free from her ponytail and fanned over her shoulders in a silken, chestnut wave. Her cheeks were flushed, lips swollen. So lovely he ached.

A frown creased her brow, and she bit her lip. "Is something wrong?"

When he didn't answer, she bunched the blanket in her fist and stared at the mat. "You're going to stop training me, aren't you?"

Yes. But he couldn't say the word out loud. Before their encounter last night, he'd had some small doubt about her submissive nature. Now, he had none. And what she needed now was comfort and reassurance. Not the raw, brutal truth of regret.

"We'll find a way around the training issue." He cringed at the meaningless platitude. No doubt Reid would be able to find a new coach, but then what? Jax lived on the road, travelling from club to club, never staying for more than a few months in one place. No attachments. No commitments.

No relationships.

No loss.

On some level, he'd thought that sex with Marcy would quench the fire that burned within him whenever she was near. But he'd been wrong. Taking her, discovering they shared similar interests, a similar kink, had only made him want her more.

He should have let her walk away.

"You think I'm sexually submissive," she murmured against his chest.

He brushed his finger under her chin and tilted her head back until she met his gaze. "I know you are."

"If I am, what does that make you?"

"I like to be in control." He smiled, trying to lighten the mood. "Especially when I'm dealing with a fighter who lacks restraint."

"You seemed to restrain me just fine." Her eyes softened, and her body melted into him.

Jax's voice thickened as his imagination ran wild. "I'd like to do a lot more than just restrain you with my hand."

She shuddered in his arms, and her cheeks flamed. "I'd like that, too."

Jax pressed a kiss to her forehead. "Why does it embarrass you? You shouldn't be ashamed of your kink. There are lots of people out there with the same needs. Lots of people who can give you what you want."

She rested her cheek against his chest. "I've always had fantasies, dark fantasies. When I first started dating, I hid them away. But the more I dated, the harder it became to hide them. I asked my boyfriends to restrain me or spank me, and sometimes even use a flogger. And they tried. Lord, they tried. They wanted to please me. But it wasn't the same. They weren't into it. They didn't understand there is more to it than just the physical act. And although you say there are lots of people like us out there, I couldn't find them."

He stroked his hand down her hair. "They are out there. You just need to know where to look."

She drew in a ragged breath and then stiffened in his arms. "I had a serious boyfriend in college. Preston. He was smart, witty, charming, good-looking. We shared the same taste in friends and music. We had fun together. But he was very straight in bed, so I locked away those fantasies and pretended I didn't have those needs."

Jax rubbed his hand up and down her back. He knew what it was like to hide his darkest desires. His family epitomized the word "uptight," but after he'd left home and stumbled on the kink scene, he'd never had to hide again.

"Then one night we went to a party," she said softly. "I don't think he knew what kind of party it was. But in every room in that house, people were acting out the very things I had imagined. It made me so … hot." She stumbled over the word and buried her face in his chest. "I don't think I had ever been so aroused. We left right away, of course. But when we got home, I told Preston what I'd been hiding. And because he wanted to make me happy, he tried.

That night, he tried everything I asked. But in the morning when he woke up…" She choked back a sob, and Jax tightened his arms around her.

"Shhh, little fighter."

Marcy took a deep breath. "He looked at me with such disgust. He told me I was perverted and sick and that I'd corrupted him. And then he left, and I never heard from him again."

Anger flared through him, and he bit back a growl. "There's nothing wrong with you, Marcy. We all have needs. Different needs. People who would judge you for them aren't worth your time. You shouldn't be ashamed of who you are. And if you want to find people who share your interests, the kink scene would welcome you with open arms."

"I don't need a kink scene," she said. "Just someone who understands me and accepts me for who I am."

"Fuck, Marcy. You have to focus."

Marcy bit her lip and slid off Jax's chest. The

last hour had been the most grueling training session of her entire career. Jax had gone from patient and understanding to abrupt and temperamental—angry, even—in the space of a night and a day.

She should have guessed something was up after their encounter. Although he'd been attentive and courteous after they'd locked up the gym, he'd been distant as he walked her to her car, giving her only a perfunctory kiss on the cheek before saying good-bye. She'd been up most of the night wondering what she'd said that had made him withdraw. Had she pushed too far? Opened herself up too much? Had her candor scared him away? Maybe he'd thought she wanted more than a casual affair, and since he was leaving in a couple of weeks, he needed to put some distance between them. Make sure she understood it was sex and nothing more.

On the pretense of getting a drink, she grabbed her water bottle and slipped out of the ring. Her stomach was twisted in a knot, and every minute she spent pressed up against his body practicing submissions made the pain infinitely worse. She couldn't take another hour. Definitely not two.

As she added a few drops of water to her already-full bottle, Reid joined her at the cooler.

"You okay?"

"Sure. Why wouldn't I be? I'm fighting in the ROC event in two weeks, and Jax has been replaced by his evil twin brother who is determined to spend the rest of the evening tossing me around the mat like a rag doll."

Reid shook his head, his face grim. "This is my fault. The minute I saw you two together in the ring, I knew I should pull the plug. In this profession, coaching and relationships don't mix. Not that it can't work, but it takes a lot of effort when you're in close physical contact all the time."

"We're not in a relationship." She sighed and twisted the cap on her water bottle. "Last night when I thought he'd raised issues he wasn't planning to tell me, things got out of hand. But it's fine now. He's probably acting the same as he usually does, and I'm just being overly sensitive. I'll get over it."

Reid studied her for a long moment. "Jax is only here for a couple of weeks and then he's going to Miami. He's got nothing permanent here. His car, apartment, even his phone were provided by the gym as part of the contract. He's never stayed longer than two months in a city. Says he prefers it that way. He wants a life without attachments or relationships."

"Reid … I know. I'm a big girl. I'm not looking to get involved with anyone."

He held up a hand, forestalling her. "If it's not working out for whatever reason, just say the word, and I'll find someone else to coach you."

Someone else? Despite Jax's sudden personality change over the last hour, she couldn't imagine training with anyone else. Jax understood her in a way no one else ever had. So why was he pushing her away?

"Thanks."

Reid tucked an errant strand of hair behind her ear, and then he swallowed. "Marcy…" He cut himself off when she gave him a puzzled frown and then dropped his hand. "Nothing. Forget it. I just don't want to see you get hurt—

in or out of the ring."

"It's nice to know you have my back."

He gave her a half smile. "I messed up real bad once. Didn't see something that was staring me in the face, and someone I cared about got hurt. I promised myself it would never happen again. So I've always got eyes on you, Marcy. Always have. Always will."

"Jax?"

Jax's head jerked up as he reached for the door handle of his rental car, a sporty Audi A4. *Damn.* No running away for him. But really, he shouldn't be surprised. Marcy wasn't a woman who shied away from confrontation, and tonight he'd given her something to be confrontational about.

He'd been a fucking bastard.

Spinning around to face her, he leaned against his vehicle and folded his arms. Aggressive? Defensive? He hardly knew himself anymore. His behavior this evening had been totally out of line, uncharacteristically harsh, and yet he couldn't stop himself. Part of him wanted to push her away so he wouldn't have to convince her to fight, when truly, he wanted her submission. Nor did he want to destroy her dreams and open his heart by telling her the truth. But the other part of him, the primal side, wanted to throw her over his shoulder and carry her off to his cave, ravage her in every way he knew how, coax her surrender, and then hold her in his arms until he had the energy to do it all again.

Unfortunately, he'd taken out his internal struggle on her.

"What's going on?" Marcy had changed into a pair of tight jeans that hugged the curves of her hips and her long, lean legs. With a short leather jacket thrown over a tank top and a pair of worn cowboy boots, her hair loose and spilling over her shoulders, she took his breath away.

For a long moment, he didn't speak, caught off guard by her frank question and wary of where it might lead.

She sighed and shook her head. "You were

brutal in there. Harsh, abrupt—"

"You weren't focused." He scrambled for a plausible explanation. "It was like we were starting from the beginning."

"You didn't give me a chance," she snapped. "Five minutes into the session, you suddenly went on the attack. Is it because of last night?"

Jax's stomach tightened when her voice wavered, and he cursed himself for allowing things to get this far, especially when he either had to tell her the one thing that might destroy her dreams or walk away.

Run away. Like he always did.

"No, of course not." Even he didn't believe his own lie.

She met his gaze with a level stare, her eyes glittering under the dim glow of the overhead streetlight. "Then kiss me," she said, an unmistakable challenge in her voice. "Kiss me and show me that what happened in the gym tonight is separate from what happened in the gym last night. Show me we can make this work."

A choice that wasn't a choice at all.

With a groan, he pulled her into his chest

and slanted his mouth over hers, crushing her lips in a bruising kiss, slaking the thirst that had burned in him since she'd walked into the gym this evening.

Marcy moaned, a deep, guttural sound that hardened him in an instant. His hands glided over her body, cupping her ass and pulling her tight against him. Blood pounded through his veins as he devoured her mouth, giving her no respite until she whimpered.

Appalled at his loss of control, he pulled away. But Marcy followed him, pressing her soft, sweet breasts against his chest, her breath whispering over his lips.

"Jax?"

No. God. No. He had to stop. It could take weeks to find her a new coach, and he would do her more harm than good if they became involved while he was training her. Tonight had been a case in point.

"Jax?" Her voice rose in pitch, and his stomach clenched with guilt.

"Fuck. I'm sorry." He scrubbed his hand over his face, as much to clear the fog from his brain as to keep his gaze off her lush lips, pink and swollen from his kiss. "I shouldn't have kissed you, and last night … and the night before, I shouldn't have let it happen."

Her breath caught, and she stared at him, aghast. "But … I wanted it all to happen. It was my choice, too."

He shook his head, jaw tight. "It's my responsibility to stay in control. You're just so beautiful, sweet. You were hurting…" His voice trailed off as the irony of the situation twisted his gut. Her success as a fighter depended on his failure as a dominant. If he stayed, he would destroy them both.

"I'm cutting the contract short," he said. "I'll talk to Reid in the morning, but I expect to be gone by the end of the week."

For a long moment, she stared at him, her body trembling. Then her eyes hardened. "Because of me."

"Because of us."

"There is no us." She folded her arms across her chest. "There is you and there is me. We did some training and had sex, but that was all. I didn't want more. You didn't want more. If you want to leave, don't make us the reason." She took one step back and then another, and then she turned and disappeared into the shadows.

Fuck.

Every instinct screamed at him to go after her. But his thoughts were too twisted up to sort through the tangle of emotions churning in his belly. He should be relieved, happy even. It was done. He'd broken it off. Reid would find her another coach, and he'd almost finished with the other fighters he'd been contracted to help. One or two more sessions and he would be free.

So why did his heart ache at the thought of moving on?

After turning down an invitation to join the other fighters for a drink at the bar, he drove back to his corporate rental apartment, furnished in bland beige and brown. Here and there, he'd tried to add his own touch: a White Sox pennant, pictures of his family, a drawing from his niece who still hadn't given up hope he would one day give her a cousin to play with, and a bottle of George T. Stagg, his favorite whiskey.

Unable to focus long enough to watch TV, he changed into his fight shorts and ran through an exercise routine in the spare room he'd set up as a makeshift gym. When even physical exertion could not calm the raging torrent of need coursing through his blood, he stripped off his clothes and stepped into the shower.

"Dammit."

He turned the shower to full blast, and as soon as the water hit his skin, he fisted his cock and began to stroke.

Eyes closed, chest heaving, he handled his cock with an uncharacteristic roughness, his hand quickening as he visualised Marcy's sweet face flushed with arousal. The gentle curves of her body. The dip of her stomach. Her beautiful heart-shaped ass, so soft beneath his fingers. His cock thickened in his palm, and he pumped harder, imagining her breasts, soft and warm in his hands, her pussy wet and ripe for him…

Fuck.

Firm now. Faster. Every stroke bordering on pain as the hot water beat down on his body. Punishing himself for drinking deeply of her honey and tasting the sweetness of her lips when he knew that banquet was not meant for him.

Oh god. Those lips.

Close. So close.

He beat himself without mercy, the slap and slide of his hand clearly audible over the pulse of his shower, the sound driving him almost insane as he imagined himself driving deep inside her.

Fuck. Fuck. Fuck. His muscles tightened, and in his mind, he buried himself in her soaking pussy, pinching her clit so they could come together in a violent, heated rush.

His balls lifted, tightened. Finally he came, his release bursting from his spine in long, heated jets of liquid pleasure as he groaned, "Marcy."

He was well and truly fucked.

Chapter Nine

"SO HE'S REALLY gone?"

Marcy's heart stuttered in her chest as she dropped into the chair across from Reid's desk. She hadn't really believed Jax when he'd said he was leaving, and when she'd seen him in the gym yesterday, she'd thought he'd decided to stick around. But the minute Reid had called her into his office, she'd known. He was gone, and he hadn't even bothered to say good-bye.

Reid scraped a hand through his hair and gave her a sympathetic look. "Jax talked to me yesterday. He said something had come up, and he had to break the contract. He flew to Miami this morning."

Stunned into disbelief, Marcy just stared.

What kind of fighter gave up after one fight? She'd had worse disagreements with Preston and, except at the end, they'd always managed to work things out. But then she and Preston had been together for years. She'd known Jax only a few weeks, and that knowing wasn't knowing at all.

"Did he leave a number?"

Reid shook his head. "He dropped off the keys, refunded the money I'd paid him, and apologized for his abrupt departure. I told him to keep the fee since he'd helped everyone through their issues, but he refused." He paused and his eyes softened. "He said he'd hurt you more than he'd helped you, stalled rather than progressed your career by telling me you weren't ready, and it was something he would always regret."

"I get it, Reid."

Reaching across the desk, he squeezed her hand. "You gonna be okay? I know there was something between you—"

"No. It was nothing. He was just a coach."

Just a coach.

Nausea roiled her gut, and she spun around and walked into the hallway.

"Marcy." She could hear the distress in Reid's voice, but she pushed open the front door and just kept walking.

✧ ✧ ✧

Marcy returned to her usual routine of days at the sporting goods shop and nights at the gym. Determined to put the problem behind her, she drilled her submissions to the point she could do them in her sleep, hauling anyone and everyone onto the mats to practice with her, but always, at the back of her mind, she worried. What if Jax was right?

After a few days as her grappling partner, Two Step offered to give her a new nickname, the Submission Master, but she refused. She didn't want anything to change. She had always been his baby girl, and she wanted it to stay that way.

True to his word, Reid hired a new coach, a gruff, retired UFC fighter named Dan. After their first training session, Dan told her she needed to stop fighting so hard and relax into submission. She'd almost laughed at the irony. She was a fighter, and she needed to do what fighters did best. Fuck Jax and his suggestion that she needed time to work through the issue. She'd been doing fine before he'd come, and with Dan and Reid working with her now, she'd turn that four and oh record into a five and oh and win herself a place in the state championships.

But alone at night, with nothing to occupy her mind, Marcy had to deal with the emptiness eating her up inside. Silly, really. She had known from the start Jax was only sticking around for a few weeks. Nothing like the years she'd spent with Preston. And yet she'd felt a much deeper emotional connection to Jax and a much deeper pain when he left. Worse, her old doubts had returned. Not even long talks with Val in the sporting goods shop or a weekend with Two Step at the youth club could ease her anxiety or her deep-seated fear that she wasn't cut out to be a fighter. Maybe her family was right, and there was nothing Marcy could do to earn their respect.

Still, it wouldn't stop her from trying. Nor would a pesky issue with freezing in submission. And after two weeks of intense training, she felt ready. She even made weight the day before the event after a few late-night ice cream indulgences to soothe the ache in her heart.

Reid picked her up the morning of the ROC event. "You think you're ready?"

She hesitated only a moment and then stiffened her spine. Doubt or no doubt, she still wasn't about to throw away her dreams. "Hell, yes."

A grin split his face as he pulled away from the curb. "You've done great this week. I think you're ready, too. If you win this bout, you still might have a chance at the championship."

Warmth suffused her body, pooled in her belly, and for the first time in weeks, a genuine smile curled her lips. "I won't let you down, Reid."

"I know you won't. You're a fighter. Always have been. Always will be. You can't change who you are, but if something is holding you back, you just gotta find a way around it. There are different ways of fighting, different ways to win."

There were also different ways to lose.

Eight hours later, Marcy sat in the ambulance outside the fight venue and wondered how she could have deceived herself to such an extent she'd deceived Reid, too. The fight had been a disaster. Just as Jax had predicted, she'd been paired up with a submission expert. She'd had to change her fight strategy on the fly when she realized her opponent was determined to get her down on the mat. Instead of taking the offensive as she usually did, relying on her strength as a striker, she was forced to defend from body slams and takedowns, backing into the ropes to avoid being drawn into a grappling match. And when she'd finally slipped up and her opponent had locked her in a quick kimura submission, she'd felt the familiar warning rush of confusion that always preceded the darkness. But this time, knowing what would happen next, powerless to stop it, she'd tapped out moments before she'd lost consciousness.

Of course, Reid hadn't been pleased. He'd been even less pleased when the ring doctor insisted Marcy get checked over by the paramedics in case she'd left it too late. And after she'd received the all clear, he wouldn't speak to her when she asked him to drop her at the after-party at Two Step's house instead of taking her home.

But Reid didn't understand. If she went home, she'd spend the night rehashing the fight in her mind, wondering what would have happened if she'd refused to be intimate with Jax until her professional issue was resolved. Could he have helped her? Even if he'd managed to do so, there was no guarantee she would have had a spot in the state championships. She'd needed this fight. But she'd needed to win. Now her record was tarnished, Reid would never support her in another event until the issue was resolved, and she was back to being alone and worried that she wasn't cut out to be a fighter.

All in all, a bad decision. Just like Jax had said.

"Hey, baby girl, need another drink?"

Marcy took the proffered beer bottle from Two Step and joined Val on the barstools at his kitchen island. "Great party," she shouted over the not-so-dulcet tones of Stereoliner. "But, as always, you invited too many people. I could barely get through your living room."

Two Step laughed. "That's what makes it a great party. And I'm expecting another wave of people now that Club Excelsior is closed for the night. Reid said he would round up any stragglers and bring them over."

"No doubt I'll know them all, and the ones who aren't already hooked up will be gay or on the rebound," Val muttered. "Seriously. I work at a sporting goods store owned by a bunch of hot fighters, and can I get some of that sugar? No. I'm stuck with accountants, middle managers, and paper pushers. If Reid doesn't have a decent straggler for me, I'm gonna give him a piece of my mind."

Marcy grimaced. Reid was the last person she wanted to see, and when she'd heard he was coming to the party, she'd almost bailed until

Val promised to keep her distracted with an endless supply of chili lime margaritas. So far so bad. Val hadn't stopped talking about hot fighters since she'd walked in the door, and the only alcohol on offer had been the one drink she couldn't stand, beer.

"You'd better get started on your margaritas." Marcy gestured to the blender. "Reid can be a tad intimidating, but not as much as me when deprived of my promised distraction."

"Heard you got dragged out to the ambulance. Maybe you shouldn't be drinking," Two Step said as Val slid off the seat and headed for the blender.

Marcy's jaw tightened. "I'm fine. They said I was fine. And if ever there was a night I needed a drink, this is it. Jax was right. I shouldn't have gone out there. Good thing he took off so I didn't have to face him." She took a sip from the beer bottle and cringed as the warm, bitter liquid slid over her tongue.

"Fuck."

"Yeah." She took another sip and shuddered. How did people drink this stuff?

Two Step lifted an eyebrow. "I meant you and Jax."

She snorted. "There was no me and Jax. That was something that ended before it began."

"Sorry. Got confused the way you two were rolling around on the mats…"

"Training," Marcy cut him off with a glare. "We were training."

Two Step laughed. "Yeah. Training. If I had a girl who looked like you lying on top of me for hours every night, I'd tell her she needed more training, too."

Marcy's breath left her in a rush. "You don't think…"

"Don't ask me." Two Step gestured toward the door. "Ask him."

Marcy didn't need to turn around. She sensed Jax behind her, felt his heat. But even if she hadn't been so attuned to his presence, Val's wide eyes and raised eyebrows would have given the game away.

"Hey, Jax. How's that cup working out for you?" Val's lips quivered with a repressed smile, and Marcy mentally crossed Val off her Christmas lists for the next ten years.

"Perfect." His voice rolled over Marcy, deep and warm, bringing back memories of their night in the gym. She pushed away thoughts of that voice in her ear, filling her mind with deeply erotic images of the things he wanted to do to her body. Instead, she focused on Val smirking across the counter, Two Step's blank expression, the steady drip of the faucet, and the gentle rattle of bottles on the counter as the heavy bass of Slayer pounded through Two Step's house.

For a long moment, no one spoke. Marcy picked at the label on the beer bottle while Two Step and Val exchanged a glance. Sure, she was being rude, but she had every right to be. Didn't she?

"I saw the fight," Jax said.

"So you came to hear me say you were right?" She stared straight ahead. Afraid to turn around. Afraid to meet his gaze. Afraid the sight of him would make two weeks seem like two minutes and she'd want him all over again.

"No. I came to speak to you about something else. Come. We'll go for a walk."

Marcy stiffened at Jax's commanding tone. Did he really think she'd go anywhere with him after he'd walked away without a good-bye?

"I'm busy right now."

"Marcy..."

"Busy."

"Actually, we're not that busy," Val said, a smile curling her evil lips. "I was just about to whip up a pitcher of margaritas, and Two Step was about to do a walk-around with that case of swill he passes off as beer." She dropped her gaze to a furious Marcy. "Maybe you should go talk to him. He's looking kinda down. Not the cheerful cup-buying Jax we saw in the store."

Kill you, Marcy mouthed at Val before turning around and glaring at Jax. "No walk. Just talk. You have five minutes."

He gave her a curt nod and followed her out to the balcony, closing the glass door behind them. A cool breeze ruffled Marcy's hair, bringing with it the faint kiss of the ocean and memories of happier times. Family times. She hugged herself against the chill and longing for the sister she hadn't spoken to in years.

Jax's brow creased in a frown. "Cold?"

"We're only here for five minutes. I'll survive."

"You don't have to just *survive*." He shrugged off his jacket, and before she could protest, he had wrapped it around her. Marcy steeled herself as the residual warmth of his body seeped into her skin. No way would one chivalrous gesture undo the damage he'd done. She gave him a begrudging thanks and then shrugged. "Say what you have to say, Jax. I was having a good time until you showed up."

He raked his hand through his hair and sighed. "I was an ass."

"Yes, you were."

"I don't do this." He swallowed and gripped the railing. "I don't usually get involved. I move so frequently it's difficult to sustain any kind of relationship."

Marcy shivered despite the warmth of his jacket. "Is that really it, or do you move to avoid getting involved?"

"Maybe a bit of both." He moved closer to her. So close she was surrounded by his scent, warm and rich, sensual. Her defenses began to crumble, and she was almost overwhelmed with the desire to wrap herself around him and hold him tight. Hold him here.

"I'm sorry," he said. "I shouldn't have left you before the event. You needed me, and I wasn't there for you. I don't know if I could have made a difference, but I could have tried. We all have different ways of dealing with challenges. Running away is mine." He cupped her jaw in his warm palm, and every cell in her body heated, locking her in place even though part of her knew the best—safest—thing to do would be to walk away.

"But I came back this time. I was there for your whole fight. I was kicking myself the whole time I was cheering you on."

"You grovel well." She leaned into his touch, and he stroked his thumb over her cheek.

"I want you, Marcy." His voice dropped to a low murmur. "Like I've never wanted anyone else before. I fucking ache with wanting you."

"Could've fooled me." She tried to keep her tone light, cool, detached, but her words came out in a breathy whisper, betraying her desire.

"I tried." He pulled her against him and bent down to brush his lips over her cheek. Marcy sighed, and he caught her breath in a searing kiss, parting her lips with his tongue to ravage her mouth, hot and demanding.

Marcy pulled away, breaking their kiss. "Not hard enough."

He clasped her hand and skimmed it down his body to the bulge in his jeans. "Definitely hard enough."

She laughed. "And here I didn't think you had a sense of humor."

"There's a lot about me you don't know."

"Tell me." Marcy pressed her hand against his erection and felt him harden under her touch. "Tell me something about you. Maybe if I knew you better, it would be easier to forgive you."

His voice dropped, husky and low. "I was the bad kid in school until my mother enrolled me in a kid-friendly MMA class at a local gym. I found a focus for my aggression and a hidden talent for beating up local bullies."

"Hmm. I like the idea of bad-ass Jax." She stroked along his rigid length, moist heat flooding her sex as she imagined his thick cock inside her. "Especially because I was a bit of a rebel, too, except I was more of the head-banging, death metal, fuck-the-world kind. Tell me something else. Did you want to grow up to be a pro fighter?" She tugged open his fly, releasing his shaft, and then wrapped her hand around him. Jax groaned.

"Marcy … not here."

With a wicked smile, she gave his cock a long, slow stroke, admiring the contrast of velvety softness over hard steel. "I'm waiting."

His ragged exhalation tickled her cheek, and he grasped her shoulders as if to steady himself. "I enjoyed fighting, but I'd always been interested in psychology and helping people deal with problems. I had to give up that dream when my mom became ill. She didn't have any insurance, and fighting was the quickest and easiest way to make money to cover her medical bills. And I was good at it. In the end, though, the money bought her a few years but not a cure."

Marcy's heart squeezed, and she quickly pulled away. "Oh, Jax…"

He covered her hand with his own and threaded his fingers through hers. "I need you. But not just like this. I want more. All of you, or at least as much as you're willing to give. Submit to me."

Wet, needy, burning with desire, she whispered, "Yes."

Countdown to crazy hot sex.

Ten minutes of chit chat before socially acceptable to leave Two Step's party without appearing: a) desperate; b) obvious; or c) horny.

Two minutes of driving before Jax demanded she remove her panties.

Three seconds to remove said panties.

Four miles of sheer terror mixed with dripping desire as Jax slid the fingers of one hand deep into her pussy while attempting to steer his car with the other.

Five flicks of Jax's thumb over her throbbing clit as she ground against his hand and begged for release.

Six refusals dropping from Jax's lips.

Seven curse words dropping from hers.

Eight floors to travel in the elevator between the parking garage and his hotel room.

Nine minutes before the building manager asked through the intercom why the elevator had stopped.

Ten fingers sliding under her shirt, unfastening her bra, cupping her breasts, and pinching her nipples until she moaned.

Eleven steps from the elevator to Jax's door.

Twelve long seconds of waiting while Jax fumbled with his keys.

And then the door opened.

Before she could blink, Jax had her up against the wall, his hand on her sternum, his thick thigh rough between her legs. The door shut behind them with a bang, and then his mouth was on hers, his tongue delving deep before he tugged her T-shirt and bra up and over her head to reveal her breasts, already freed from their restraint in the elevator.

"Stop." She drew in a ragged breath, then

scored her fingernails down his shirt until she reached the hem. "What about yours?"

"Can't wait." With a sharp yank on her ponytail, he jerked her head back, exposing her neck to the heated slide of his lips. Then he latched on to her left breast, drawing her nipple into his mouth, sucking and nipping until she was writhing against him.

"Need to touch you, Jax." She tugged at his belt, her little finger skimming over the steel of his erection beneath his fly.

With an irritated growl, he grasped her hand and tugged it away. "You don't touch unless I say you can. Especially now. I won't last if you wrap that sweet hand around me again."

"What about if I do this?" She ground her hips against his jean-covered shaft, smiling when his cock hardened between them.

"My little fighter's being a naughty girl." His eyes gleamed in the dim light. "How should I punish her this time?"

Marcy stilled, scarcely dared to breathe, as he pulled yet another fantasy from the darkest recesses of her mind. "I thought you said you couldn't wait. No time for punishing naughty girls."

"Changed my mind. Turn around." He spun her to face the wall. "Skirt off, then hands on the wall. Legs spread. I know exactly how we'll keep you in line."

His feet thudded over the carpet as he walked across the room, decorated in ultra modern white and more white. From the bedding to the curtains and from the carpet to the furniture, not a smidgen of color marred any surface, like an untouched canvas, a snow-swept montage.

Marcy slid her skirt down over her hips, kicking it off her ankles and toward the front door. Then she took up her position. For the first time ever, she felt totally and utterly vulnerable, exposed. But, curiously, not ashamed.

Moments later, Jax returned. She sensed him behind her, although she hadn't heard his footsteps. He glided his palm around her waist, pulling her against the bare expanse of his rock-hard chest. Anticipation ratcheted through her, and she trembled.

"Do you want to play, Marcy?" he murmured. "We haven't discussed limits, but I would love to see how you respond to a belt or a flogger."

"God, yes." She turned her head and kissed his cheek, shivering when his five o'clock shadow scraped against her heated skin.

His hand slid over her hip and along the curve of her sex. Then he thrust one thick finger deep into her slippery entrance. Marcy cried out as arousal flooded her veins.

"So wet, and we've only just started." He chuckled softly, pulling away. "Stay still and don't turn around."

She heard the clink of a belt buckle followed by the unmistakable slide of leather. *Oh god. No.* Looking back over her shoulder, she tried to find him in the shadows. "Jax—"

"Eyes forward."

She turned her gaze back to the wall, and suddenly he was covering her with his body, his chest pressed against her back, his heat soaking into her skin, his scent enveloping her. Soothing.

"Does the idea of being spanked with the

belt scare you?" His breath was hot and moist in her ear as he kicked her legs apart, sending streaks of white lightning straight to her core.

"Yes," she whispered. "But it isn't a limit for me."

"A belt can be used for pleasure," he murmured as he slid the doubled thickness of the belt between her legs, brushing the cool leather along the curve of her hot, wet sex. "Or pain. But you aren't ready for that type of pain. Not yet."

A thrill of fear shot through her, and she moaned at the deliciously erotic sensation of hard leather pressed against soft flesh. But her relief was short-lived. Jax dropped the belt and trailed the soft suede ends of a flogger down her arms.

"Has anyone used a flogger on you?"

Marcy swallowed hard, her gaze riveted to the soft black tails caressing her arm. "Yes. Once. But he was too gentle with it." Now there was an understatement. Preston had wielded the flogger like a feather duster, barely touching her skin, tickling her until she wanted to scream with frustration.

He brushed the flogger over her hip, down her stomach, and then wiggled the tendrils over her bare sex. Marcy tilted her hips, seeking more sensation as moisture flooded her pussy.

"I won't be gentle," he said softly. "But I won't go hard. Not as hard as I suspect you'd like. Definitely not hard enough to send you into subspace. That's something we have to work up to. I just wanted to give you a taste. Gauge your reaction."

"Punish me?" She couldn't keep the hopeful note from her voice.

Jax laughed. "Oh yes. If that's what you want, I'm more than happy to punish you. Do you remember your safe words?"

Marcy swallowed past the lump in her throat. "Red to stop. Yellow to slow down. Green to keep going."

"Perfect. Now brace yourself."

She barely had time to draw in a breath before she felt the soft thud of the flogger against her ass, a gentle pressure as if he was pushing her forward. He repeated the stroke on her other cheek, and then he started a soft, sensual rhythm, pausing only to brush the tips of the tails along her soaking folds.

Marcy's body heated as he increased the pressure. Although her body registered pain, the sensation quickly morphed into pleasure. She cried out as need, fierce and unrelenting, crashed over her in a pulsing wave.

"Use your safe words if you need me to stop," he murmured as he struck her again.

She inhaled deeply, breathing in the rich scent of his cologne—of him—and tried to steady herself. But despite her best efforts, a violent shudder shook her body, drawing her precariously close to climax.

"So responsive." He smoothed his hand over the flaming skin of her ass and then followed the cleft to her folds. Slicking her moisture up and around her clit, he groaned. "God, Marcy. Knowing this gets you off … you don't know what that does to me."

He pulled away and struck her with a slow, steady rhythm that left her panting and aching with need. Her limbs turned liquid as sensation chased away all rational thought, spinning her away…

No. She wasn't spinning. Or flying. Instead, she was cradled in Jax's arms, safe and warm as he made his way across the room.

"We have to stop." He spoke softly, half to himself. "I've already gone further than I wanted to go. I never imagined you'd respond so well."

"Please, no…" She didn't want him to stop. A fog hovered at the fringes of her consciousness, the promise of emotional release, a place where nothing mattered. She wanted him to take her there. Set her free.

He made love to her instead.

Gently, tenderly, he laid her on the soft down duvet covering his massive bed. As he stripped off her clothes, she caught glimpses of DIY and fight magazines strewn across the carpet. Protein shake tumblers and fight gear spilled out of the suitcase on his dresser.

Before she could ask any questions, his fingers skimmed over her abdomen, sending a renewed burst of endorphins singing through her veins. His hand followed the curve of her sex to stroke her wet entrance, and Marcy trembled under his touch, her questions giving way to the throb of desire between her thighs and the slide of cool silk over her burning skin.

"Jax, please."

But he was in no hurry. He knew just how far he could take her, teasing her with his fingers, his lips, his tongue, stopping before she reached her peak, until she burned to have him inside her, out of her mind with need. And when he finally covered her with his body, slid his cock into her aching center, filling her completely, something shifted in the air between them. She lost the coach and found the man.

"Oh god." Her breath caught as her inner walls stretched to accommodate him, a delicious pain. "You feel so good. Perfect."

"I dream of you." He dipped his head to nuzzle her neck. "When I'm in the shower, in bed, even running in the morning, I imagine you're with me." He inhaled deeply and nipped the sensitive skin between her neck and shoulder blade. "I catch your scent on my shirts, and it drives me crazy."

He angled his hips, pulling out and then plunging even farther than before, ripping a gasp from her throat. She bit her lip at the exquisite sensation of having him so deep, buried to the hilt, connected to her in a way no one else had ever been, body and soul.

"I wanted you the moment I saw you." He deepened his thrusts, his cock swelling, hardening with every stroke. "And as I got to know you, I wanted you even more."

A bubble of emotion rose in Marcy's chest, and she choked back a sob, even as she writhed beneath him.

"Tell me what you want." His hand drifted down between her thighs, his thumb circling her clit. "There isn't a need you have that I don't want to fill."

Desire, deep and dark, curled inside her, winding through her body like a ribbon. "Take me," she whispered, lifting her hips to ease his way in. It was all she had to say. From the way his eyes glittered, hot with sensual promise, she knew he understood.

"I'll take you. Every way I can get you." He

quickened his strokes, pinning her to the bed with each drive of his hips, letting her know there would be no escape unless he allowed it, no release until he gave it to her.

And he did. He hammered into her hard and fast, carrying her body to its peak with an unyielding relentlessness that took her breath away. With firm, gentle pressure, he stroked his thumb over her clit, and she came in a searing burst. Shattered. Heart, body, and soul united in overwhelming pleasure.

Acceptance.

As he followed her in release, she wondered what it would be like if he stayed in Seattle.

With her.

Forever.

It didn't take long for the panic to set in.

He held her for an hour after he'd made love to her, and for fifty-five of those minutes, he was hard. Again.

If they were going to take their relationship further—and for the first time in ten years, he wanted something more than a casual affair—he'd be the one setting the limits. Marcy wanted it all—every sensation, every experience, everything he had to offer. She submitted with a trust that humbled him and a willingness that frightened him. His gut tightened with guilt. A relationship was based on mutual trust, and he had been keeping a secret from her far too long.

He shifted on the bed, and Marcy stirred, lifting her head and gazing at him, her eyes still heavy with passion.

"Do you still doubt you're sexually submissive?" He stroked a hand along her back, and she dropped her head to his shoulder.

"No." She spoke so quietly he almost didn't hear her, but he caught the hesitation in her voice.

A wave of protectiveness washed over him as she nuzzled his neck. He had to tell her the truth. Not just because it was the right thing to do but because he couldn't stand by and watch her throw herself into a fight that could very likely lead to serious injury, even death. He hadn't been able to save his mother and sister, but he could damn well save Marcy. And then he could take the relationship forward with a clear conscience.

"It could be that the sexually submissive aspect of your personality is holding you back in the ring." He swallowed past the lump in his throat. "When you're forced into a submission, your natural instinct is to submit instead of fight. I saw it the first day we met, and I don't think it's something training will be able to overcome. Given who you are, you may not have what it takes to ultimately succeed as a fighter."

For a long moment, she didn't move, didn't speak. His heart pounded in his chest, and when she stiffened and rolled away, he knew he'd made a mistake.

Maybe the biggest mistake of his life.

"I can't believe you're only telling me this now." She wrapped the sheet around her and slid off the bed, and her voice took on a bitter tone. "All the time you were training me, you never believed I would succeed."

Jax's throat tightened. He had waited too long to tell her the truth, breaking the trust before it had even had a chance to take root.

"Did you know that was my biggest fear?" Her voice wavered as she searched for her clothes. "That I wasn't really cut out to be a fighter? That I really was the failure my family believed me to be?"

"You're not—"

She cut him off with a shake of her head. "You said what you had to say. Too damn late."

While Marcy dressed, Jax tugged on his jeans in silence, uncharacteristically at a loss for words. Helpless in a way he hadn't been since the death of his sister. But when she stalked toward the door, desperation loosened his tongue. "Wait."

"You're wrong." She spun to face him, her eyes glistening with unshed tears. "You think you know me, but you don't. You've seen only the tiny piece of me I allowed you to see. We've fought and we've fucked, but we missed the part in the middle where I tell you all about me, and you tell me about you. You don't know I bake cookies when I'm stressed or that I bite my nails when I'm sad. You don't know I have a sister I haven't spoken to in years and who I miss desperately. You don't know that my favorite season is winter or that I'm into Thrash, or that I cry at airports or that my favorite thing to do is watch bad movies…" She paused and drew in a ragged breath, then stiffened her spine and swallowed.

"Marcy…" He took a step toward her, his stomach clenching when she backed away.

"And I know very little about you," she said bitterly. "You keep your cards close to your chest. Even in your suitcase"—she waved her hand vaguely across the room—"there's hardly anything that tells me who Jax is, what he likes, what makes him laugh or cry, what makes his heart sing—"

"You, Marcy. You make—"

Marcy shook her head, cutting him off. "I made a mistake trusting you before I really got to know you or let you get to know me. I thought I'd make it as a fighter because of you. But now I'm going to succeed despite you. I'm going to prove you wrong. Regardless of what you think is my true nature, I'm a fighter. I'm going to fight to beat this problem. And I'm going to win. But I'm going to do it alone."

Chapter Ten

When Pam "the Punisher" Jones broke her arm trying to escape a kimura in an illegal underground smoker fight in the Menlo district, two things happened. First, she had to drop out as an alternate in the state championships. Second, Marcy squeaked into ninth place on the alternate list for the state championship. She needed one more win for a place on the list, and Reid knew a promoter who owed him a favor. The next day, Marcy's name was on the card to fight in National 60's big event.

Marcy had always thought she'd been training hard before, but the hours she'd spent in the gym were nothing compared to the hours Reid now demanded in the month-long lead-up to the event. The Callaghan brothers gave her a leave of absence from the store to train, and she moved in with Val to save on rent. Val was more than happy to have the company, especially when Marcy's fighter friends started hanging around their place.

Part of her new training regime involved seeing a fight psychologist she'd found after an exhaustive search, but after a few sessions, Marcy had called it quits. Although she was able to help Marcy understand that there was nothing wrong with her kink, without any actual fight experience or a willingness to get in the ring, she wasn't able to help Marcy deal with her problem in practice. In short, she wasn't Jax.

And Jax was still around.

He had tried to call her after she'd fled his hotel room, even stopped by her house, but even after he'd apologized, Marcy had made it clear she wasn't interested in seeing him again. She'd expected that was the last she would see of him, but Jax had other ideas.

Two week after their breakup, he showed up at the gym as Club Excelsior's head coach.

When confronted by an irate Marcy, Reid explained he had decided to cut back on coaching and focus more on the administrative side of the business, and when Jax had approached him about working at the gym, the opportunity had been too good to pass up. Jax now had a rental apartment a few blocks away and had bought Reid's old Jeep. He'd cancelled his contract in Miami and the rest of his contracts for the rest of the year for the sole purpose of being there for Marcy in whatever way she allowed him. According to Reid, he'd realized he had been wrong about her, and this time, he wasn't running away.

Although Reid had assured her he would stay as her coach as long as she needed him, Marcy wondered if she should start looking for a new place to train after the National 60 event. Seeing Jax every day was a stress she didn't need. Not only was it difficult to move on, the effort involved in avoiding him was taking its toll on her both mentally and physically. Jax respected her wish to be left alone, but she knew he was watching, and that, more than anything, made it impossible to erase the memories.

Had she been too harsh? Had her reaction been more about receiving a message she didn't want to hear—and didn't believe—rather than about receiving it too late? Over the next six weeks, she found herself watching him with the other fighters, remembering what it was like to have him on top of her, teasing her, drawing out her deepest desires and bringing them into the light. He had given up a lot for her, come back to make amends. Maybe she could open her heart just a bit to forgive him.

The night before the big event, Reid pronounced her ready, and Marcy agreed. She felt ready. Not only that, for the first time, she didn't feel ashamed of who she was. Whether she won or lost, she would always be a fighter. And if she had a submissive side, she would fight that, too. But only in the ring.

After leaving the gym that night, she called her sister, Mel, for the first time in five years. They had always been close, but after she'd turned her back on Wall Street, where Mel now worked as an investment banker, they had drifted apart. She realized now it was because of her. If she'd accepted herself, maybe her family would have accepted her, too.

She told Mel about her career as a fighter and about the upcoming event. She'd never expected Mel to say she was proud of her. And she couldn't hold back her tears when Mel said of course she'd be there to cheer her on.

Friday night. Fight night.

Marcy's heart thudded in her chest as she climbed into the ring. Seattle's KeyArena was packed for the National 60 event, and she tried to focus on the opponent in front of her instead of the glaring lights, the cheering crowds, or her sister in the front row beside a grinning Two Step.

And Jax was here. Although she couldn't see him, Reid had told her he was in the crowd, and she was grateful for his presence. Knowing he believed in her and cared enough to give up his career to try and make amends made her feel warm inside, supported in a way she had never been at home. Loved.

Diane "the Demolisher" Bowman, so named because she had won most of her fights by knockout, warmed up in the opposite corner. Although they were evenly matched in weight, Bowman was taller and leaner with a long reach. But more than that, she was a known submission expert.

Marcy and Reid had studied Bowman's technique all week, looking for weaknesses and ways to escape her brutal submission holds. Although they had made a game plan, Bowman was known for pulling off unexpected moves, and Marcy had prepared herself to improvise.

The first shot of adrenaline hit when the bell rang. Just as well. Bowman was quick off her feet, taking Marcy's back and attempting to sink a chokehold. Marcy resisted, and Bowman turned it into a neck crank, tightening her grip. Marcy fought furiously, but the more she struggled, the tighter Bowman held on, and Marcy knew in her heart she was going to freeze.

"*Yield to me.*" The words whispered through her mind, and for the briefest second, she thought she saw Jax at the side of the ring, arms folded, legs apart, his favorite admonishing position. She closed her eyes and thought of the moment she had given him everything and how, for those few seconds, she had felt free.

No. Jax had encouraged her to fight the submission. She twisted and flailed in Bowman's arms, raining useless blows as her air supply slowly dwindled.

Yield.

Maybe that was where Jax was wrong. Maybe, instead of fighting who she was, she should accept it and use it to her advantage.

So she did. And as her body relaxed into the submission, an overconfident Bowman loosened her grip.

Heart pounding at the unexpected opening, Marcy managed to untangle Bowman's body lock and shake her opponent free. The crowd roared in approval. Gripping her opponent in a headlock, she rained punches on Bowman's head and shoulders before setting up an arm bar. Bowman struggled against Marcy's hold, alternating fists with brutal elbows, and as the round ticked down, she worked herself free. Finally slipping Marcy's hold, Bowman spun around and knocked Marcy to the mat in a brutal double leg takedown, quickly locking Marcy in a triangle. But this time, Marcy was ready. Taking a deep breath, she slammed her way through and pinned her opponent until the time ran out.

After the bell, she helped Bowman to her feet, and they waited, breathless, for the judges' decision.

Bowman on points.

"I'm sorry," she muttered over the cheering crowd as Reid helped her out of the ring. "I messed up. I thought I had it, but she turned it around."

He wrapped her in his arms and squeezed her tight. "*You* turned it around. Fucking brought a tear to my eye when you broke that submission. Next year, you'll not only make the championships, you'll be going pro. Guaranteed."

She'd waited for him. Knew he was there.

Jax paused midstride when he caught sight of Marcy leaning against the ring in the near-empty arena. Her hair was loose, just dusting over her shoulders, and she wore a simple white sheath dress that hugged every curve of her lush body.

He had tortured himself for the last few weeks imagining his hands on the gentle curves of her hips, the soft swell of her breasts, the lush ass that had borne his marks when he'd walked away. What a fucking mistake.

Not only that, he'd been wrong about her. She was twice the fighter he was, and deep down, she'd believed in herself in a way he never had.

Swallowing hard, he closed the distance between them. "Good fight."

"I lost."

"Not to me. Not to Reid. Not to you." He could hear the husky edge in his own voice. Raw. Broken. "You rocked that submission, Marcy. Nothing's going to hold you back now. You're going all the way."

His heart hammered in his chest. He ached

to hold her, but he could read her well enough to know he had to keep his distance.

"Reid said you stayed for me." Her voice wavered, and a sliver of hope shot through his heart.

"At first, I thought I couldn't coach you to fight the submission when it was the antithesis to what I love about you sexually. I couldn't separate the personal and the professional, and I didn't think you could, either." He forced himself to hold her gaze although part of him wanted to look away from the accusation in her glittering eyes. "But when you walked away, I realized you were right about a lot of things. I didn't know you, and I hadn't made the effort to get to know you because I was afraid of getting more attached than I already was. But you knew yourself. You knew your strengths. You just needed to accept who you were. And so did I."

She closed the distance between them and reached up to stroke his jaw, a light touch and one he couldn't read. But he could feel her heat blazing a trail across his skin, and his throat tightened with need.

"You grovel well. I know that much about you."

In that moment, he knew he would never be able to walk away again. With a soft laugh, Jax cupped her face between his hands and tilted her head back to meet his gaze. Her eyes were warm, accepting. Forgiving.

"I need you, Marcy. More than I need to protect myself from losing someone again. I want to see where this takes us. Seattle is a permanent move for me. The first time in ten years I've ever wanted to put down roots. Even if it doesn't work out, you've given me the courage to put the past behind me."

A smile tugged at the corner of her lips. "Why do you think it won't work out?"

He pulled his cell phone from his pocket and tapped on the screen, then held it up for her to see. "Reid asked me to pass on a message. One of the fighters on the alternate list dropped out. Even though you lost the last two fights, your record is still better than Bowman's, so you get her place. You're going to the state championships, Marcy."

Her breath caught in her throat, and she threw her arms around him. "I can't believe it. I thought I'd have to wait another year." And then she pulled back. "But why do you think it means things won't work out between us?"

"'Cause I'm head coach now," he said, his voice laced with amusement. "Means you train with me and Reid, and I won't have it any other way. And when one of my fighters has the state championship within her grasp, I give it everything I've got. You're gonna hate me by the time the championships roll around, but dammit, you'll be good. I'm gonna be tough on you. I won't hold back."

"Inside the bedroom or out?" She pressed a kiss to his throat.

"Both."

"I can hardly wait."

THE END

Thanks for reading *Yield to Me.* I hope you enjoyed it!

If you are interested in finding out when my next book is available, please sign up for my new release newsletter at www.sarahcastille.com, like my Facebook page at facebook.com/sarahcastilleauthor or follow me on Twitter at @sarah_castille.

I appreciate all reviews, positive or negative. Please consider leaving a review on Amazon, Barnes & Noble, Goodreads etc. to help other readers looking for books.

For more sexy MMA fighter romance, try my Redemption series:

Against the Ropes (Redemption #1)
Publishers Weekly Top Ten Pick for Romance & Erotica and #1 Erotic Romance Amazon Bestseller

In Your Corner (Redemption #2)
Publishers Weekly Best Summer Reads (Romance) & Starred Review

Full Contact (Redemption #3)
Coming Soon

If you would like to read an excerpt from *Against the Ropes*, please turn the page.

Excerpt from Against the Ropes (Redemption, #1)

He scared me. He thrilled me. And after one touch, all I could think about was getting more…

Makayla never thought she'd set foot in an elite mixed martial arts club. But if anyone needs a medic on hand, it's these guys. Then again, at her first sight of the club's owner, she's the one feeling breathless.

The man they call Torment is all sleek muscle and restrained power. Whether it's in the ring or in the bedroom, he knows exactly when a soft touch is required and when to launch a full-on assault. He always knows just how far he can push. And he's about to tempt Makayla in ways she never imagined…

Excerpt from Chapter One…

Run. I should run. But all I can do is stare.

His fight shorts are slung deliciously low on his narrow hips, hugging his powerful thighs. Hard, thick muscles ripple across the broad expanse of his chest, tapering down to a taut, corrugated abdomen. But most striking are the tattoos covering over half of his upper body—a hypnotizing cocktail of curving, flowing tribal designs that just beg to be touched.

He stops only a foot away and I crane my neck up to look at his face.

God is he gorgeous.

His high cheekbones are sharply cut, his jaw square, and his eyes dark brown and flecked with gold. His aquiline nose is slightly off-center, as if it had been broken and not properly reset, but instead of detracting from his breathtaking good looks, it gives him a dangerous appeal. His hair is hidden beneath a black bandana, but a few tawny, brown tufts have escaped from the edges and curl down past the base of his neck.

A smile ghosts his full lips as he studies me. A lithe and powerful animal assessing its prey.

My finely tuned instinct of self-preservation forces me back against the ropes and away from his intoxicating scent of soap and leather and the faintest kiss of the ocean.

"Excuse me…Torment. I…thought you forgot to buy a ticket, but…um…I don't think you really need one. Do you?"

"A ticket?" His low-pitched, husky, sensual voice could seduce a saint. Or a young college grad trying to supplement her meager salary by selling tickets at a fight club.

My heart thunders in my chest and I lick my lips. His eyes lock on my mouth, and my tongue freezes mid-stroke before beating a hasty retreat behind my Pink Innocence glossed lips.

He steps forward and I press myself harder against the springy ropes, wincing as they bite into my skin through my thin T-shirt.

"Are you Amanda?"

With herculean effort, I manage to pry my tongue off the roof of my mouth. "I'm the best friend."

He lifts an eyebrow. "Does the best friend have a name?"

"Mac."

"Doesn't suit you. Do you have a different name?"

"What do you mean a different name? That's my name. Well, it's my nickname. But that's what people call me. I'm not going to choose another name just because you don't like it." My hands find my hips, and I give him my second-best scowl—my best scowl being reserved for less handsome irritating men.

His gaze drifts down to the bright white "FCUK Me" lettering now stretched tight across my overly generous breasts. With my every breath, the letters expand and retract like a flashing neon sign. I hate my sister.

He leans so close I can see every contour of bone and sinew in his chest and the more intricate patterns in his tribal tattoos. The flexible ropes accommodate my last retreat, and I brace myself, trembling, against them.

"What's your real name?" he rumbles.

"Makayla." Oh, betraying lips.

He smiles and his eyes crinkle at the corners. "Makayla is a beautiful name. I'll call you Makayla."

Heat roars through me like a tidal wave. He likes my name. "So…about that ticket—"

Want to read the rest? *Against the Ropes* is available in all e-book formats, paperback and digital audio.

Other books by Sarah

The Redemption Series (Erotic Romance)

Against the Ropes

In Your Corner

Full Contact

Fighting Attraction

The Legal Heat Series

(Erotic Romantic Suspense)

Legal Heat

Barely Undercover

Burnout

The Sinner's Tribe Motorcycle Club Series

(Contemporary Romance)

Rough Justice (February 2015)

Beyond the Cut

Steel Heart

The Club Excelsior Series (Erotic Romance)

Yield to Me

Hold to Me (coming soon)

Promise Me (coming soon)

About the Author

New York Times and *USA Today* bestselling author Sarah Castille worked and traveled abroad before trading her briefcase and stilettos for a handful of magic beans and a home near the Canadian Rockies. She writes contemporary and erotic romance and romantic suspense for Sourcebooks Casablanca, Samhain Publishing, and St. Martin's Press. Her stories feature blazingly hot alpha heroes and the women who tame them.

Connect with Sarah

Website:

http://www.sarahcastille.com

Facebook:

http://www.facebook.com/sarahcastilleauthor

Twitter (@sarah_castille):

http://www.twitter.com/sarah_castille

Goodreads:

http://www.goodreads.com/author/show/6920675.Sarah_Castille

Pinterest:

http://www.pinterest.com/scastilleauthor

CPSIA information can be obtained
at www.ICGtesting.com
Printed in the USA
FSHW020810020220
66739FS